ANTHONY CRONIN

THE LIFE OF RILEY

BRANDON

This edition published in Ireland 1983
by Brandon Book Publishers Ltd,
Dingle, Co. Kerry.

First published by Martin Secker & Warburg Ltd 1964

Printed and bound in Great Britain by
Redwood Burn Limited
Trowbridge, Wiltshire

The Life of Riley

Also by Anthony Cronin

Poetry

Poems
Collected Poems
Reductionist Poem
41 Sonnet-Poems 82
New and Selected Poems

Prose

Dead As Doornails
The Life of Riley
Identity Papers
A Question of Modernity
Heritage Now: Irish Literature in the English Language

Drama

The Shame Of It

Preface

THIS APPARENT account of about two years of his life was found among the late Patrick Riley's socks, rags and papers after his death. I have undertaken the task of presenting it to the public with mixed feelings: even the mere handling of the manuscript had its problems. It will be seen that the narrative is, so to speak, open at each end. Quite an amount of further material remains in my hands, and I hope, Deo volente, some day to publish the bulk of it. However, in so far as the separate character of this particular manuscript is any guide, Riley apparently intended it to have some unity and significance of its own; and I have concluded therefore that it should so stand. It is almost entirely self-contained; and, from an editor's point of view, it is, quite frankly, of a handy size.

If I may introduce a more personal note, I would like to say that the task of reading and editing the manuscript has for me been a strange one, since I knew Riley on and off during the period he describes, though we mixed in different circles and I was concerned—if that is the word—with other, though sometimes adjoining, matters and enterprises. Hence I never became acquainted with any of those among whom his fortunes were tried and his endeavours used. I have yet debated with myself whether to add a cautionary, or emendatory, or explanatory word here and there; but have decided, I hope rightly, that it is better to let the dead speak for themselves.

ANTHONY CRONIN

AT THE time of which I speak I was working for a crowd of grocers, being known as the Assistant to the Secretary, a title which conveys, and was meant to convey, a distinct inferiority of status. In the early days, when I had been, if not exactly enthusiastic, at least humbly hopeful to please, I had signed myself a few times, Assistant Secretary. This was partly out of a desire for order and convention: I had heard of Assistant Secretaries, but never of such a thing as Assistants to the Secretary, and I hate ambiguity of status. However, I was not allowed to get away with it for long; and my efforts to define my position in what I understood to be orthdox and easily explainable terms were now only a blunder in the past, to be used at moments, with great sarcasm, by the Secretary himself.

The grocers all had Ford Prefects and all carried large Players—it was before the days of Senior Service. They were small grocers and dairymen of a type now, I think, passing. My man the Secretary was of course not a grocer, but a professional agitator and rabble-rouser who had banded the grocers together for his own interests. He was a smooth, shaven-jowled rascal with horn-rimmed spectacles and a full-lipped, down-turned mouth, the picture of an executive genius except that the arse of his breeches was inclined to hang a little loose. This characteristic may have been deliberately adopted, however, for it was universal among the grocers, and like many great statesman, my man was a master of the common touch. His technique was to impress them at one moment with the complexity, rarity, and ultimate loneliness of his intellect; and at the next with his plain, ordinary, honest-to-goodness, horse sense. He gave them to understand that into the dark places that he knew, no ordinary man could follow; that he was the lonely possessor of a mind which weighed every problem sleeplessly and balanced and counter-balanced every possible philosophical implication; but this once done, he conveyed, no man could better steel himself to the necessity for action. Once the decision was taken he was calm, passing round the large Players and swopping scatological stories with the best of them. I have often wondered about that baggy arse to the breeches since, and decided, on the whole, to give him credit for a masterly minor detail.

The grocers' primary object, of course, was to prevent each other opening on Sunday mornings or knocking three-farthings off the pound of sugar; but to hear him talk to them sometimes one would imagine that he had in mind a sort of Academy of Grocing, a strict, austere and incorruptible body who wore cocked hats on state occasions and endowed orphanages, encyclopaedias and research projects. He varied this line of chat with a lot of hard-headed stuff that he knew to be ultimately nearer their pockets, but their pleasure in both was evident; he knew the mixture, if any man did, and he indulged them to their hearts' content.

Once a week the grocers' committee met in plenary session in the inner offices, and this night was my particular torment. There was barely time to slip out for three or four pints between the end of the normal working day and the time when the Ford Prefects began to arrive. There were ten or a dozen of them on this committee, all of course on Christian name terms with each other and with my man the Secretary. I was the only mister in the room and they were all misters to me.

They would stand around the table for a while, their breeches bagging at the arse, offering each other the large Players before getting down to business. Frequently cigaretteless as I was, I would have to stretch my already taut nerves still further in my attempts to get close enough to a group to intercept a Player or two.

"Well, Jim, how are things out in Harold's Cross?"

"Ah musha, can't complain, I suppose. Can't complain."

"Business good?"

"Could be worse for the time of year." Eyeing his competitor narrowly: "They tell me you have a new Home and Colonial up your way."

"Ay, they've bought the site. Used to be Murphy's the hardware. Doyle's corner."

"Soon be handin' out the stamps. Free electric razor with every half ounce of tea."

"Well begod we'll have to see about that, won't we? That represents a threat to us all. Meehaul"—this was my man the Secretary—"Meehaul's the man for that."

"Ay, Meehaul's the boy to put a stop to that if anyone is. Stamps on the agenda this evening, Mr. Riley?"

Agendaless, and rarely consulted about the agenda, I would experience slight panic. Stamps were usually there, but it would be foolish to take a chance. "Don't you have a copy, Mr. Mullagh? Hold on."

I snatched one from the table, eye and brain frenziedly searching.

"No. 5. Distribution of gift-stamps by chain . . ."

"Yes, as a matter of fact they are. Mr. Murphy"—that was the Secretary—"Mr. Murphy's very worried about them."

I caught his eye upon me: patent hostility, mixed with contempt. Had I said something wrong? Was it a gaffe to suggest that the great man could actually be worried about anything? As so often, I realized my political deficiencies.

"Yes, we'll be having a word or two about that, Sam," the statesman himself interjected, grave of demeanour, the weight of the issues showing in his eye, but still unflappable, the will in control.

"The Chairman and I might have to ask you to give up a little of your time to join a deputation to the Minister."

This was good stuff, as even I knew. Deputations to the Minister were calculated to give any man a sense of his importance, not only in his own eye but in that of the wife and neighbours.

"How's the missus? Was that the eldest lad I saw in the papers got his leaving cert?"

"It was, thanks be to God, Meehaul. I might put him on for the civil service. He's a good lad, a good lad."

The Chairman, Mr. Paddy Boggins, was by way of being a bit of an intellectual, and it was my misfortune that he had once come upon some verses of mine in a magazine. Sooner or later during the course of these preliminary sociabilities he would shout down the table, "How's the poetry going, Mr. Riley? Are you gettin' any inspiration this weather?"

It may, for all I know to this date, have been meant well, but it was accompanied by a leer so blood-curling that all possible answers—had there been any—were consumed in shame; it invariably resulted in humorously indulgent looks from the bystanders whose cigarettes I had been snitching and in whose conversation I had been attempting to join after my broken fashion with the casual but reserved good fellowship which was the Secretary's stock-in-trade. As for the great man himself, he generally stared at me through his horn-rims for some seconds after the remark had been made: silently, speculatively, coldly, impassively one might say except for a slight exaggeration in the down-turn of his rather full lips. Oh, he had crosses to bear—I will be the first to admit that; and he had long since given me up as almost hopeless.

Not that he was not by way of being an intellectual himself. Far from it. *The Economist, The New Statesman, The Trumpet* were forever on his desk; and he subscribed I knew to one of the better-known book clubs; at least it was an easy matter to collate his reading with their advertisements. In the early days, on our way perhaps to an audience with the Minister, or a conference with the Vincent de Paul Society about the provision of rainproof clothing for messenger boys under nine, he used sometimes to engage me in conversation about the early works of O'Faolain, or Aldous Huxley, or Negley Farson. I even think it may have been my perhaps rather distant attitude to the works of these masters that first began to alienate him. I was aware too that he frequented a public house where the opinions of these authors, of *The New Statesman* and of other progressive organs were canvassed by the clientele (mostly the more intellectual type of civil servant or the secretaries of other organisations, the retail bicycle traders or the registered pork butchers) through the medium of the Gaelic language. You know the type.

The tasks I was required to perform in the course of assisting the Secretary were not beyond the powers of a man of moderate health and capacity. I should have done better, I know. Yet there were a variety of factors, which I hope to describe as far as possible without self-pity in a moment, preventing me from letting loose the full powers of my will and energies, such as they were, on the job. The result was of course that I was unhappy in his service. It seemed to be always light and airy sunlight outside the office, so that one was filled with a fierce desire to look at the sky through the window of a pub instead. Once in the pub, however, it seemed to be always raining, so that a return through the greasy, cold and dreary streets to one's place of shame and torment seemed more agonising a prospect than ever. Somewhere a process of demoralisation had set in, and once that starts Assistants to the Secretaries, whoever they may be, are on the slippery and downward slope which can only end in disaster. Oh ye Secretaries of this world, take care that those who assist ye shall not suffer the first pangs of demoralisation, for the first once suffered, there is no arresting the disease.

It was not of course that I was incapable of formulation of policy, or that the policy decisions I made turned out to be wrong; that, for instance, I favoured pressure on the government to prevent price cutting, or that he thought it sufficient to blackmail the wholesalers into boycotting the offenders, and that he turned out, as usual, to be right. On such matters of high policy I was not encouraged or required to form an opinion at all; though I will admit that I often pretended to be a policy maker when talking to obscure and ignorant grocers out of his earshot, indeed often gave a passable imitation of the great man himself and, such is human nature, enjoyed doing so.

Nor were my duties of a particularly obnoxious kind. It is true of course that I often had to play my tiny part in ruining men who for all I know weighed out as honest a pound of sugar as the next, and had daughters at the Dominican Convent, Wicklow; it is also true that I had to assist, however humbly, to prevent messenger boys forming themselves into trade-unions; but where is the job, in the modern world, which does not require the shutting of one's eyes to certain moral imponderables in the interests of one's employers? Oh Fleet Street, instruct me, now and forever, amen. One of my duties was to act as a recorder of what passed at committee meetings, general assemblies of the full membership of the organisation, conferences with the Minister, with the trade unions and other bodies. I know that to pass one's life recording the opinions of grocers (and every man who had an opinion on anything expected it to go into the minutes) is not a task of boundless excitement and reward, but it is not too onerous to be borne. Also I was required to answer members' queries on the telephone or by letter about government regulations, the law relating to grocing, wholesale prices, the official policy of the association, and other matters about which I knew nothing but was expected to find out, and, worse still, to care. I attribute my frequent inability either to find out or to care both to the factors I shall presently attempt to describe, and to one, small, immediate circumstance, slight in itself maybe, be perhaps determinate in the long run. This was the fact that I sat with my back to my man the Secretary's door. In the throes of dictation; on the telephone; during the perusal of documents, in the course of my private affairs, my back was vulnerable. It was, somehow, much worse than it would have been if the threat had been sideways on, or straight in front, or diagonally perhaps to the left or right. It was not the silence or the secrecy of his approach that unnerved me so much as the fact that his eyes were upon me for some seconds before I saw him. Imagining that look of ferocious speculation, of murderously dispassionate enquiry, was somehow much, much worse than actually encountering it. You may well ask why I did not move the desk, and indeed I have asked myself often enough since. I think the real reason is that it just did not occur to me that the thing was movable. It was the first time that I had actually lived in intimacy with one of those large office desks that have drawers right down to the floor (God, what went into those drawers) and I really believe I thought the thing was a fixture, bolted or built into the planks. Anyway though, I was never allowed that much initiative in anything, and I dare say the attempt would have been a failure. He was not a man to forfeit such advantages lightly.

Sitting there with my back to the door was terrible. When the Secretary man arrived—he was always extremely late, which he claimed was his privilege and alleged would not be mine in years to come unless I could be on time now—he would storm through into the inner office, brief-case, baggy pants, horn-rims already ablaze with determination to make everybody pull their weight. According to oft-repeated instructions I was to let ten or twelve minutes elapse before I followed him into that inner office behind my back. During this time he was, or so his secretary told me, at stool, but I think myself that the stool part of it was merely a cloak for a form of meditation on my iniquities, past, present and to come. Then I would gently and timidly enter, on tiptoe, with the morning's mail in hand. It was my duty to have read these letters, and it was the practice to hand them to him one by one with a brief resumé of what they appeared to be about, plus, if possible, some sort of a comment, not always easy to think up. What should have happened then was that he would toss, say, roughly seventy-five per cent of them back to me, with either some signal of agreement with my comments or some suggestions of his own. In fact he was rather cleverer than that.

I would hand him, say, the first letter, mumbling something about it meanwhile. He would peruse it for a while, apparently attentive to its contents. Then he would place it flat on the desk in front of him and gaze sternly and scornfully through his horn-rims, through my non-horn-rims, into my eyes, drumming his fingers on the letter the while like a man desperately trying to contain his patience.

This never failed to work. For Christ's sake, I would wonder, had I handed him the wrong letter, dismissing as a mere enquiry about tea-rationing a communication from the Minister himself? Or was there potentially explosive matter in the wretched document that in my ignorance I had missed? But no.

"What time did you arrive this morning?"

"Some time after half-past nine."

"Some time after half-past nine. I'm perfectly well aware you didn't arrive before half-past nine. How much after half-past nine?"

"About ten minutes, or maybe a quarter of an hour."

"About ten minutes, or maybe a quarter of an hour. And do you know what might have happened during that ten minutes or maybe a quarter of an hour? The Chairman himself might have rung up with an urgent query about . . . about gift stamps, or tea rationing, or, or next week's conference with the Minister even."

There were tears in his eyes, of frustration, of anger, of the wounded trust of the great of this earth who must forever carry their immense burdens alone.

"And do you know what would have happened then? *I* would be in trouble for failing to see that *you* did *your* job. And do you know why you're supposed to be here? Not because you could answer the Chairman's query about tea rationing—and the Chairman I can assure you knows that all too well, you needn't run away with the idea that the Chairman is under any illusions about that—no, because this office is supposed to be at the disposal of members from half-past nine onwards. And if the Chairman does ring up to ask somebody like you a question to which he probably knows the answer perfectly well, and knows furthermore that you do not know the answer, he is simply ensuring that if another member rings up during business hours he will find somebody here besides the"—he waved towards the office where the typists brewed tea—"the women. And if you continue to come late in the mornings, they will begin to come late in the mornings; there will be nobody here even to answer the telephone, the place will be locked, bolted and barred when the Chairman rings up, or perhaps even attempts to effect an entrance in person if it should so happen that his affairs take him this way, and in his wisdom he decides to call. I cannot take all the responsibility for everything all the time. You are in a position of responsibility also. When I am not here the conduct of the affairs of this association devolves upon you. It is for you to set an example to the women. It is for you to be here when and if the Chairman or any other member rings up. And it is my duty to see that you are here at whatever cost to you or to myself."

At the mention of his responsibilities he closed his eyes

and assumed an expression of immense weariness. I was to understand that the man I saw swopping stories and Players with the committee was a mere façade: little they knew, little I knew, little the women knew, the ultimate loneliness of high office and how much depended on this one man.

Then the telephone would ring. Slowly his eyes would open, slowly his hand reach out, pause in mid-air, and then decisively descend. All at once the mask would be assumed again; the voice, cheerful, relaxed and assured, would greet the unknown interrogator.

"Hello? Indeed it is. Indeed it is, Bill. O not too badly, not too badly. Bearing up like us all. Well now I'm glad you rang, because I was on the point of asking you to give up a little of your valuable time to have a word with me about that. Not that it's too serious because as you probably well know the act does not empower them to issue a directive. But it's as well to be forearmed eh?"

With his free hand he would sort through the letters, toss a pile of them at me and wave me to the door, crooking his leg over the arm of the chair meanwhile, the very picture of confidence, bonhomie and decision; and, it might be added, the strongest possible contrast to my sorry self.

For the rest of the morning I would sit with my back to his door, eliciting information or misinformation from the civil service and other organisations in answer to the queries in the letters. Then I would begin to dictate my replies to one of the secretaries that we Secretaries and Assistants to the Secretary were provided with, struggling to formulate answers that would conceal my ignorance and to concentrate my thoughts on what I may call my epistolary prose rather than on the symmetrical little rump and sharply jutting breasts that passed my desk several times a day.

Sooner or later during this operation the door behind me

would silently open and the statesman would emerge. He would pause and I would know of his presence only by a flicker in the eyes of the—let us call her the stenographer, there are too many secretaries present—and the soft but menacing sound of his breathing. My prose would begin to falter.

"It appears that regulations require that non-perishable goods . . . that non-perishable goods should not only be sold, should not only *not* be sold rather but should not be exposed to be sold, I mean for sale . . ."

The statesman would now have come into view, perhaps gazing sombrely out of the window, as if waiting for a word with his assistant, but wishful not to interrupt.

" . . . during the permitted hours, I mean the hours that are permitted for the sale of perishable goods but not non-perishable goods if you see what I mean . . ."

Desperately floundering to regain a hold on a subject already slippery enough in all conscience, I would go from bad to worse, while the clouds gathered over the statesman's face and he turned to stare at me: speculatively, with interest, with dogged attention, with his mouth turned down. Finally, with a "when you're quite finished, could I have a word with you?" he would disappear whence he had come.

There were of course brief, though as a rule very brief, intervals of sweetness and light between us. In the early days there were the passing references to O'Faolain and Negley Farson, thrown out to show that the man of action was also a man of culture, like a renaissance prince; but I speak now of something more personal and intimate, when the great man, pleased perhaps by my conduct in some small matter, my way of accepting a cigarette from the Chairman, or my look of attention as, pencil poised, I waited for the remarks of Mr. Phonsy Mulroney of Terenure, would cast aside the robes of office for the moment and permit himself reminiscence, or general reflection or fatherly admonition.

I would be squeezed in beside him in the Ford Prefect perhaps, while he negotiated it past a drove of bullocks on our way to or from an arbitration tribunal, when he would begin: "I've been in public life now for upwards of a decade . . .", or, "Let me give you one solitary word of advice. . . ." These occasions were as I say rare, and they became increasingly so as the harvest of my crimes grew and the drawers of that accursed desk accumulated rubbish and unanswered letters through the long summer days, but they continued spasmodically into the autumn of our relationship, and I never ceased to be moved by them. One line of chat he continually returned to, but since I confined myself, overcome as I was, to bare nods, or "I sees", or gestures of assent with the Player he had just offered me, I never quite made out what he was talking about.

He would begin something like this.

"Cigarette? No, no, I have matches somewhere. H'mm. Let me give you one solitary word of advice. Later, when you're established, and if you pull yourself together"—a penetrating look—"you'll become established, you'll have time for this and that, you'll be able to do as you please outside of office hours, to do as you please within limits, to divide your energies. For the moment you've got to remember that you're beginning, and the start you make now, the impression you make now, is going to decide your future. Holy God, man"—this impatiently, but certainly friendly "Holy God, man, we all have to begin. We all have other interests. But at the beginning we all have to concentrate. We all have to live with the job. We have to cut down on other things. Later on, if you pull yourself together now, you'll find you have time for, for all sorts of things. I had to begin myself, so I know what I'm talking about. And you've got to remember that if I got run over by a bus in the morning, you'd be the man in possession, dependent on the impression you'd made on the Chairman you could very well step straight into my shoes."

Touched as I was, I used to wonder what on earth he could be talking about. Was it my unfortunately discovered activities as a versifier, or my all too obvious hangovers, or something darkly mysterious, far beyond the last fling of the imagination, which was presumed to pre-occupy me to the detriment of my capacities? Or was it simply that he envisaged me as, like himself, a subscriber to the well-known book club, and was suggesting that if I held my horses for a while that and discussions of the opinions of *The New Statesman* in the sweet and kingly tongue would be all very well, would indeed become my office and my fame, but at the moment represented a dangerous diversion of energies?

WHATEVER it was, it was far, I think, from the facts. My agonies at an end for a few brief hours I would make straight for a pub called O'Turk's, an establishment which, whatever its merits or demerits, had a mental atmosphere in stern and refreshing contrast to that prevailing in the grocers' headquarters; or indeed in that other establishment where the Secretary discoursed in the tongue with his fellow Secretaries, Permanent, Under, Departmental, and simple, like himself.

For the key and cardinal principle of O'Turk's was gurrierdom. Here not success, but unsuccess, was looked upon with favour. Here the man who made a hames of it and continued, whatever the obstacles, to make a hames of it, was the man of fashion. Hence O'Turk's had a high proportion of beggars, and of successful and well-to-do beggars at that, not ordinary, common or garden, public-house touchers.

Of course not everybody could set up as a beggar. There had to be a history of sacrifice or misfortune or oddity to enable one to qualify. And here there were distinctions not readily apparent to the outsider. Plain congenital idiocy would not do, for a beggar was expected to be a sharp fellow and if possible a wit: but a maladroitness in affairs amounting to an inability to hold any ordinary employment and preferably having resulted in the loss of a sum of inherited money or the destruction of an inherited business at some time in the past (or, what was equally good, the repute of it) would. Patriotic service in one of the extremist organisations which had flourished in the thirties and in the war years was a splendid qualification for the role. But this was tricky ground; for not only was it difficult to distinguish between extremist patriotic activities and several other offences known to the law, but it was not difficult for the unqualified to invent an extremist present about which they were naturally sworn to secrecy. And there were in fact a number of outrageously ignorant but quite voluble marxists who belonged to a neo-Communist organisation, in fact seemed largely to control its destinies, though why this should have debarred them from other employment than that of beggar in the pub was not made clear. This overcrowding and this confusion rendered the extremist role a tricky one to adopt, though it was admitted on all sides of course to be a proper qualification. Literary and artistic preoccupations were also, in a way, accounted sufficient, though here again there were snags. It was better, for the true beggar, not to have published or painted anything at all, for to do so smacked almost of having a job, and one was more likely to be begged from than permitted, by the necessary common consent, to beg. Conversely of course a degree of literacy was required, or an ability to pretend to it: I mean common literacy; it was difficult to pretend that one could write if it was known that one could not read.

There were other qualifications—anarchism, Zionism, having been charged with murder or one or two other recognised offences, even if one couldn't pretend to a patriotic motive—but indeed, as in everything else, fashions came and went. The fashionable beggars of one month might be patriots; of the next, poets; so that it was customary to pretend to several factors disabling one from earning what is called an ordinary living and play up whichever seemed most profitable at the moment, subject, as I say, to such inherent obstacles as a degree of illiteracy so gross that it obviously disbarred one from the role of literary man, or a spastic condition so extreme that it patently prevented one from claiming to be a notorious killer.

The difficulty in the economy of this particular pub was to preserve some sort of a reasonable balance between the number of beggars and the number of non-beggars. The disparity did not have to be as great as might at first appear necessary. For one thing, not all of the beggars were whole time: they occasionally stole, or succeeded in backing a winner, or laying their hands on a portion of the funds of an extremist organisation, or at least on a portion of its postage stamps. On these occasions it was politic to be free with the proceeds, in order to preserve some shred of that most valuable of all reputations in Ireland: "He doesn't often have it, but he's dacent when he does." Further, strokes of good or bad luck were constantly driving people up and down the scale; and surrounded by such evidence that the will to work might vanish overnight, or the muse call to a sterner discipline than mere money-making, or the political conscience prod a man to abandon the ways of mammon, and his consequent sufferings for the good cause possibly incapacitate him forever, most of those who had were quite willing to give: either to placate the gods, or through respect for what was deemed to be a higher way of life, or because they had formed a secret resolve to take to beggary themselves in the near future. Besides, O'Turk's was a famous pub where company was to be found at all hours of the day, and while the number of beggars or part-time beggars and steamers might be equal at any given time, the steamers, in fulfilling the duties of their employment, had to go and come. I must add that the beggars were themselves great travellers, constantly on the road between Dublin and London, their route being traditionally the cattle-boat to Liverpool and the King's highway from there. As Yeats said of the writer, freedom to travel at any moment was the one privilege their trade allowed. Small troubles, the desire for change or for a rest from the pub, minor spiveries, the wish to avail themselves of the facilities afforded by the welfare state, the presence of one or two O'Turk's outposts in London, were all contributory to the general restlessness. It was a poor man indeed who could not raise the fare to Liverpool and there was little or no difficulty in making one's way from there.

This is a work of history; and the reader must beware of categorising what I describe in the nomenclature of another day. The company which frequented O'Turk's in the late forties was, I suppose, bohemian enough; but would hardly have merited from certain latter-day exponents of the theory and virtue of bohemiansm, the accolade of the words beat or hip. Nor indeed would the more old-fashioned word bohemian itself have occurred to many to describe their mores, their circumstances or their state of mind. A man who pretends to read electricity meters for a living, but who spends most of his time in the pubs making entries in his dockets according to what he presumes to be the law of averages, may be square or beat or hip according to another's point of view, but according to his own is simply beating the rap. A thief after all, if one leaves out the morality, is simply a shopkeeper without a shop. Suffice it to say that the motley throng which sat around the pub begging or being begged from were not remarkable for honesty, trustworthiness, truth, punctilio, delicacy, scrupulousness, punctuality, dignity, respectability, sobriety, purity, decency, modesty, chastity, continence, cleanliness or shame; that those of them who earned an honest living did so unwillingly, sullenly and without ambition unless by ambition is meant the desire to get one's hands into the till; that not a few of them earned their living dishonestly and a considerable number did not earn it at all, honestly or otherwise.

Besides the beggars there was a fairly considerable smattering of small *rentiers* and one-time gentlefolk, those who were in receipt of, or in touch with the annual income (seldom less than four hundred pounds, and hereinafter in this chronicle referred to as the Protestant Four Hundred) that is the right of every Anglo-Irishman from birth. Most of these presented themselves not as distressed gentlefolk, but as engaged in activities either directly artistic, such as lino-cutting, ornamental fretwork, or versification, or ancillary to the arts, such as bee-keeping, collecting folk-songs, exploring their Oedipus complexes or having deserted from the Royal Air Force. They were flanked by a small number of pure English whose incomes were as a rule larger but less certain, being dependent on the whim of a blind old mother in Bath, or a trustee in Cheltenham, or a junta of disapproving brothers and sisters in Bradford; and whose avocations were roughly similar. Both these groups favoured the polo-neck, the baggy flannels and the tweeds which were authorized everywhere as the uniform of the bee-keepers, lino-cutters and folk-song collectors of the day.

Associated with them were the Japanese and American geniuses who commuted between Dublin and Paris. These mostly favoured the novel as a means of expression or an excuse for having or not having money, and the duffel-coat, then in the first bloom of its civilian popularity, as a symbol of caste and status. All these groups were important insofar as they had women, which were in short supply, and cash, which was in even shorter, and was perhaps the more important commodity of the two. In fact all three, plus the natives in regular employment, provided that nucleus of cash upon which vast superstructures of idleness can surprisingly be erected, but without which they are impossible to maintain. Though in the case of the Japanese and the Americans, it must be added, it was very difficult to ascertain precisely how much they had, for some were rumoured to be rich beyond the dreams of avarice, others were genuinely penniless, or had been so since the G.I. Bill of Rights folded up; and one and all masked for opposite but complimentary motives, their enormous wealth or their utterly abysmal poverty behind the same façade of genius.

There remain the natives. Something has already been said about the beggars, their military and revolutionary ardour, their impracticality, their rumoured but crippled talents. There was also a numerous riff-raff of auctioneers, insurance salesmen, time-keepers, motor mechanics, warned-off solicitors, actors, scene painters, dramatists, bookie's runners and such like, depressed in spirits, not very often in possession either of their full faculties or of ready cash.

And there were too the deserving poor, a category all to themselves, and it must be added (I think I should at this stage point out that much of this information should be carried forward in the reader's mind to provide the necessary background for the next stage of my career, and to save us the trouble of vulgar explanations) a not unimportant source of cash. These were the working class.

The vague left-wingery which infected the whole ensemble, cast on the so-called working class an aura of great interest, particularly, it need hardly be added, interest to the limeys, for left to themselves the natives would be unlikely to have known that there was anything exciting, by mere virtue of his job, about a carpenter, a plumber's mate, or a stoker in the gasworks. Not that the limeys conceded that to be these things was in itself quite enough: they gilded the lily, so that the plumber's mate was invested with anarchist opinions and presented with the works of Bakunin; a turf-cutter, innocent of any ambitions other than acquiring (without, if possible, the cutting of turf) a sufficiency of drink, was gradually hypnotised into being a left-wing dramatist manqué. Of course it would sooner or later occur to even the least avaricious or most obtuse of turf-cutters that it was the best of his play to keep it up. For this reason there was a constant coming and going between the ranks of the respectable poor and the beggars; for, like a soccer player or boxer who is doing rather well but still holds on to his original job just in case, it would sooner or later be clear to the man concerned that he could not only afford to turn whole-time professional, but might even make a big career out of it. And of course he was often mistaken, or mistook his moment, or discovered too late that he hadn't the talent; or that the profession of the whole-time beggar concealed underneath a superficial idleness and freedom from care a good deal of nervous tension and plain hard work. In general it was too true that it was during the months preceding the leap into whole-time beggary that your turf-cutter or plumber's mate was most prosperous. What with lashings of free drink, Connemara sweaters, and editions of Marx or Bakunin being showered upon him he had little or no use for his own money and was as a general rule ready, in needy company, to be exceedingly free himself with the drink and the cash.

THOUGH there were others in this motley throng in somewhat similar position to myself, it could hardly be said that I frequented the right sort of pub, or frequented it in the right sort of way for the tender ambition of removing the stigma " to the " from between the words " Assistant " and " Secretary ", to flourish twenty-four hours round the clock; but my whole way of life outside of office hours was against it, from the moment I left the office, beaten and bedraggled, in the evening, to the time I returned to it, beaten and bedraggled, in the morning.

I lived in an underground system known as The Warrens, in a Georgian Square, a system which at one time had formed the kitchen and cellars of the large Georgian mansion, built in the severe but sunny Dublin classical style, overhead. The upper part was given over to the better type of dentist, who fortunately did not live on the premises; the lower, the system of which I speak, was owned—was leased rather—by an English gentleman known as Sir Mortlake who had acquired it during the war at a merely nominal rent. Sir Mortlake, like many a nobleman before him, was penniless; but he had the simple bravery and acumen that is often a characteristic of those with his sexual proclivities. His principal source of income was the nightly parties that he gave in The Warrens. Not that he charged admission—far from it, indeed, for his object was to encourage as many people as possible to come. Those who came brought Guinness. Leaving the pub they were charged on the bottles, which they naturally left in The Warrens when they went, and it was from the return of these empties that Sir Mortlake derived his modest but fairly regular income. Six dozen—and on a weeknight it was seldom less, on Fridays and Saturdays often more—at twopence on the bottle was as near as made no difference to four pounds a week, and four pounds a week plus the ministrations of those maternal women who will always be found to knit or cook for solitary, unattached, exquisitely mannered queers of Sir Mortlake's age, enabled him to live, as indeed he had a right to, like a gentleman of leisure but straitened resources. The attraction of Sir Mortlake's parties was that The Warrens were deep underground, and, the dentists being all at home in the suburbs snug in bed, the extraction of teeth by other methods created no disturbance to the public whatever. Besides it is a law of life—or at least a necessary consequence of the licensing laws in these islands—that a man who lives alone and has no objection to human nature and who keeps, nay advertises, open house will rarely be short of drink and company after the pubs are closed.

Sir Mortlake's other source of income was more orthodox but in the long run more troublesome; and, what was worse, it created, as other sources of income will, a conflict of interests. Being lord of several underground acres he naturally let out rooms or portions of corridor to other people. The Warrens consisted mostly of underground passageway, but there were rooms—former wine-cellars, kitchens, pantries and the like of that—mostly windowless and all pervaded by that smell of mouldering plaster and damp flooring brick which clings, like the ghost of money itself, to the underground portions of mansions from which the moneyed have long since departed or been driven. The trouble about Sir Mortlake's activities as a party-giver and as a landlord was that he could never be sure—at least he could never get the other party to admit—in which capacity he was acting. Naturally a fair proportion of those who came to drink remained to sleep in the passageways; and quite a number of the beggars who came to drink every night remained to sleep every night, considered themselves indeed to have established a sort of squatter's right, so that there were constant altercations on that head. It must be said, however, that it was only when Sir Mortlake, having made a rough check of the bottles before retiring, discovered some missing in the morning, that he really got angry; and, it must be said also, with some reason. All in all his activities as a landlord were a comparative failure, whereas his activities as a host were a comparative success.

I myself occupied a windowless cellar off the main passageway. It was a retreat which had attracted me from the moment I first saw it: the musty smell, the fact that harsh daylight, for a period of almost two hundred years, had never penetrated there, the sense of having returned to something like one's beginnings, primitive, close, cavernous, forgotten.

But let me not pretend that these poetic considerations alone dictated my residence there. I seemed to be unwelcome, for a multiplicity of reasons, to the ordinary type of landlady, so that I was forever having to move on; I had acquired it at a time when I was so afflicted with debt, and debt moreover which was not a matter of mere conscience or prestige but of instant and terrible gaol, that the prospect held out by Sir Mortlake of owing him the first four weeks' cash and paying thereafter the rent plus a small sum as interest—an arrangement which, I know not how, seemed to result in me paying vastly more than was agreed on—was a great attraction. Still, it only came to fifteen bob a week; and considering what I was paid for assisting the Secretary, I really do not know how I could have lived anywhere else.

However, as far as the latter consideration was concerned, it had definite disadvantages. Supposing, bethinking me perhaps of my desk and the door behind it, of the palsied, ague-ridden walk to the grocers' headquarters in the feverish mental atmosphere of the early morning, of the interminable struggle with the tea-quota system, of the fact that I would have to wear my shirt inside out for the third day running, I decided to have, at long last, a quiet night.

Then I would bend my steps home to The Warrens; make my way through the gaunt and cavernous kitchens where once the venison had roasted and from whence the gallons of boiling water had ascended to make my lord's punch; lock myself into the tiny, windowless cellar which once contained his lordship's port, and now contained my palliasse, three odd and dirty socks, a volume called the *New World Bible* and a broken alarm clock set upon the floor.

It was my custom on those occasions to crawl into bed and anneal my spirit with those Asiatic texts in the New World Bible, which spoke slightingly of the world's ambitions and employments, which suggested retreat and privacy and contemplation as the supreme goods, which counselled the uprooting of ambition and the moderation of desire. The affairs of the grocers, the ambitions of my man the Secretary, the worldly imperatives of his threats and his counsels, belonged to the world of illusion, of baseless hope, groundless fear, terrors and fevers which were fortunately, according to the New World Bible, as unreal as they were unnecessary to endure. Thus I would prepare myself for sleep, if sleep I could; thus would I strengthen my spirit for another day of abuse and my yearning to be done with it all forever.

Of course not being the man to resist temptation in any shape or form whatsoever, the advent of Sir Mortlake's guests, to the number of sometimes a hundred or more, and rarely less than a score, with copious supplies of Guinness, would disperse my drowsy meditations, or my slumbers if I had achieved them, and replace my desire for spiritual oblivion with a nagging urge to avail myself of the somewhat more accessible kind produced by alcohol. It would not be long before I had pulled trousers over my pyjamas, if pyjamas I had, and was out there among the chiefs of staff and the Japanese geniuses and the general riff-raff of the pubs, baying away with the best of them.

The sort of gathering which Sir Mortlake entertained on a typical night in the cellars underneath the once aristocratic square, while his cat crouched watchfully in a corner and the moon drifted carelessly on through the narrows of the clouds, has already been sufficiently described. Emerging from my meditations or my slumbers in my cavern I would forget for a while the cares of Murphy's office and join in the general, and, for the most part, innocent hooliganism with a will. I cannot, I'm afraid, promise the reader any hair-raising revelations of life underground in the late forties. The reefer, flower of a less fastidious time, was unknown, and if it had been known would indubitably have been scornfully rejected in favour of plain porter. There was, as I remember it, a dogged desire on the part of all hands, those who had paid for the drink and those who hadn't, to get as drunk as possible in the shortest possible time. There were renditions of familiar and generally acceptable party pieces, ranging from Sir Mortlake's "Three Old Ladies Locked in the Lavatory", to a one-armed patriot's somewhat inaccurate version of Emmet's speech from the dock. There was a general swill and a general deterioration, amid shards of broken glass and gouts of Guinness and occasionally blood, from conviviality into moroseness and from song into sleep. The interest, if any, of this chronicle, does not lie in its account of doings and disgraces of an unusual or a shocking order; nothing occurred that the imagination cannot all too easily encompass, and little I fear, except mass drunkenness, occurred at all.

I HAVE said that women were in short supply, and so indeed they were; not, of course, in the city of Dublin and its hinterland, for, as has been often enough remarked, nature has blessed the island of the Gael with a plentiful rainfall and a plenitude of personable females. The shortage lay rather in the circles in which most of those present spent their leisured, in fact their waking hours. To the number of those Gaels whose women would no more have ventured into such circles than they would into an orgy of a more overtly sexual order must be added the number who had no wish to bring them; and to them again must be added the army of beggars who could under no circumstances have maintained a fancy woman of their own, independent of the general supply, and who quite properly refused to give up their leisure in the probably futile hope of obtaining one. Some of these beggars were respectably married and supported large broods of children on the proceeds of their craft, but among them, as among the rest of the native stock in general, the Celto-Iberian order of things prevailed: the woman closeted in an atmosphere of domestic fecundity, while the man went abroad in search of converse, social and otherwise.

In short, on this part of the sea-coast of bohemia, if bohemia it was, a heterogenous collection of males had been washed up with an insufficient supply of women. That there was difficulty in recruitment from the outside may be attributed not only to the innate respectability or chastity of the females of the race, but to their fastidiousness as well. The general atmosphere was one of gurrierdom. If the general atmosphere had been one of unrestrained art, girls might have been attracted in greater numbers, but the atmosphere was rather one of thievery and chicanery, modified by art and frequently masquerading as it, not the sort of atmosphere for which a well-brought up girl who had any sense at all would abandon her bourgeois prejudices.

Nonetheless, of course, women there were, some of them

quite charming. And the shortage was alleviated in part by a sort of community spirit. The trouble was that the younger, the nicer, to the romantic eye the more likely a focus for emotion, the girl might be, the more likely she was to have been specially imported and to be held monogamously by one of the richer members of the community: unless a man were possessed of immense initiative, cash, and its attendant mobility and grace, his chances were limited. Recruitment from outside among the unattached natives was practically impossible; much of such recruitment as there was came from abroad, already accompanied by a Japanese of great wealth; such females as were available to the unattached could no longer gratify the aesthetic sense of possession after difficulty, to say nothing of the Herod complex, with its preference for youth.

This situation, which I trust I have made clear, added further confusion and duplicity to my much fractured life. The circle in which I moved, though through the exigencies of thirst and the licensing laws fairly self-contained, maintained some contacts with the outside world. Only a few could retreat into it entirely, as into a hermitage, and I was naturally enough acquainted with some females who could not be prevailed upon to spend the entire evening in the pub and the night in The Warrens. Among these was a girl called Bridget, a student nurse for whom and with whom I had formed an attachment, if attachment it could be called. She was young, prejudiced, receptive, suspicious, admiring and, within her clearly defined limits, passionate. Her attitude towards me varied from a sort of tremulous and bewildered tenderness to disconsolate anger. She was the dark-haired, large-eyed, full-lipped Irish type, what is aptly called a blooming girl, with splendid physical endowments in early maturity and possibly a hint of flesh later on. She laid down rigorous conditions for our relationship and was strong enough to impose them: but then I am easily imposed on.

Wild horses would not drag her into O'Turk's; indeed it was difficult enough to prevail upon her to enter other, more orthodox establishments, and once in she was continually agitating for a move. Her sense of public-house time was rudimentary, and of course she had absolutely no terror of the licensing laws and of the night which cometh when no man may drink. She was avid for attendance at the cinema; while my clothing preserved a certain standard she liked drinking coffee with me in public places; she even besought me angrily to go dancing with her. If O'Turk's was unpleasant and boring, the Warrens was undoubtedly the resort of the devil. I brought her there for privacy one afternoon, and thereafter, under no circumstances at all, even in the hours of daylight, would she set foot in it; and she was continually exhorting me to leave that terrible place.

She herself lived in a sort of hostel with fifty or sixty of her fellows, a kind of virginal beehive, full of song, and gossip, and rinsing noises. Past its portals I was, needless to say, denied entry, not only by her but by the authorities who guarded its stores of sweetness for subsequent lawful possessors. It will be seen that things were circumstantially difficult; I had, so to speak, to conduct a battle without a battlefield. On top of this I was frequently penniless; perennially thirsty; often in the shakes, and, while in her company, denied an adequate opportunity of a cure.

Of course she had her difficulties too. Nothing her all-seeing, all-fearing pastors and guardians had told her had prepared her for an object like me. Her armoury, her wisdom such as it was, her guile, were deployed against an enemy who, with the best will in the world, was not real, who vanished into gross improbabilities and preposterous difficulties at the drop of a handkerchief. Meanwhile, sulkily, tenderly, angrily, passionately even, she yielded and resisted. In doorways in the bitter winds of April, in the hollows of the Phoenix Park and on Howth Head above the sea and the rhododendrons she granted tendernesses which, muddled though they might be, were touching to the spirit and gratifying to the flesh, consenting often to catch her death of cold and plunge into breathless intimacies whose spasmodic abandon was real enough, though she never abandoned, indeed clung with equal fierceness to, those final defensive combinations of limb and cloth in which as a wrestler she was blindly and instinctively skilled.

She had no objection on those occasions to what passions I was shaken or taken by, nor to their rudimentary consummation. She was a good girl in that respect. But in spite of my descriptions of the bliss that lay in store for her also, if only she would allow me to finish the matter off properly, she was adamant in her refusal to enter unknown territory where putative social as well as certain moral disaster might lurk. She had been warned against this in terms subtly but terribly different from the injunctions delivered against the embraces she permitted, which, after all, though seriously disapproved of by her pastors, were to some extent permitted by the customs of the race. And for all I could in justice bring myself to believe, viewing the situation as a whole, and my situation in particular, the dear thing may have been right.

Meanwhile, in the scented darkness of cinemas she snuggled closer while the film and the licensing laws fought out a parching finish before my eyes, or tenderly and often humorously eyed me over the cup that cheered but alas did not inebriate. It must not be thought that because I was denied what I presumably—for the whole situation was so erratic that I scarcely know—most desired, that I got no worthwhile erotic satisfaction at all. Far from it. My intimacies with her body and her clothing, though perhaps fleeting and fragmentary, were nonetheless intense; and all her youthful properties, her lips, her hair, her intumescent parts, carried to the end for me a glow of desirability and a gratification to the touch and taste which coloured considerably my preposterous days.

At the same time I must admit that the whole thing was a strain on the nerves and on the health. Those who know the withdrawal symptoms attached to spending every third evening or so more or less cut off from adequate supplies of alcoholic drink, after spending the other two swilling down everything in sight, will bear me out when I say that the accruing torments are among the worst known to man, and the night the darkest endurable. De Quincey, an expert on an analogous subject, points out that the road to health and a rosy old age is to maintain the dose: settle on what circumstances will allow and thereafter, wind and weather permitting, neither increase it nor diminish it. Further, Bridget caused me a good deal of unnecessary labour in the way of scraping up money in mid-week in order to play the role of escort to places I had no desire to frequent. I imposed on her financially it is true, but I had to have independent means to nip through lavatories and round corners for quick ones in strange pubs where I had no credit. Also she put pressure on me, much of it in indirect ways, through silences, half hours of stony abstraction and indifference, obscure forebodings which suggested imminent disaster for me and, by reflection, public obloquy for her; some of it more direct—the comments of her colleagues on my appearance and reputation, questions as to what I intended to do with myself, and whether I intended to keep this kind of thing up forever, direct exhortations to "for God's sake have some sense". Not many practical, cut and dried suggestions were made in the course of all this, but there was an undercurrent of obscure but unwearying propaganda for an amalgam of middle-class virtues which was distinctly trying on the nerves, almost as bad in fact as having another, if spare-time job.

I might have borne these drawbacks with more equanimity of soul, and blundered on after whatever will o' the wisp I sought with more single-minded perseverance, had I not been involved contemporaneously with somebody else, a lady who occasionally frequented O'Turk's and attended Sir Mortlake's parties. She belonged to the element held more or less in common, for, though not completely free with her favours, neither was she altogether reluctant to oblige a selected circle. Of late, however, that circle had shown a rather terrifying tendency to narrow down to me. She was an American and a great lover of the arts. Such was her love for them in fact that she practised the lot: she was poetess, painter, folk-song collector, folk-dancer and anything else that happened to take her fancy for the moment. No longer exactly in bud—indeed, not to put too fine a point on it, not exactly in flower—she regarded sex also as a cultural activity, the enjoyment of which marked us out as intellectuals and choice spirits far above the common herd. Her propaganda in this, as in other respects, was the exact opposite of Bridget's.

Tall, with a curious collection of bead-hung dresses which she manufactured herself—it was one of her media—a smile which for sheer desperate effulgence and understanding rivalled those of her country's politicians, a modicum of cash and unlimited energy, she had arrived on Ireland's hospitable shores with certain fixed ideas, taken an apartment and proceeded to put them into practice. Cardinal to her programme was the notion that although the Irish had all the virtues that the modern world lacked, they were in need of sexual reclamation. I think she was inclined to be disappointed in this respect until she met me.

I did not find her altogether unattractive as a person. It is true that she battered me with poems, both her own compositions and selected pieces from the works of the masters, and that her enthusiasms, if one had listened to them, would almost have sufficed to kill off the whole heritage. However, she had warmth of a sort; and she was moreover—and let this not be held against me—good for an odd plate of hot scoff and an occasional ten bob note with which to whip around corners when on a date with Bridget. She was good of course also for what every young man is presumed by cultured females of her type and age to desire, and on grounds of general improvement to need, most of all. Yet somehow the pleasures to be obtained from Eunice's embraces were not so sweet as those that beckoned mutely but persuasively in Bridget's comparative inaccessibility and in the blood.

She attacked. She handled one roughly. Her person, her motions were altogether lacking in privacy. There was really nothing to unveil. And the illusion she yet demanded of any sort of progression and conjunction was usually hers, and meant hard work on the part of her coadjutor and a stern effort to maintain readiness in face of the indelicacies of her approach. And what one entered eventually, through the floodgates of her response, was neither so close nor so intimate as one could have wished. I do not wish to seem ungallant, but there was that about her that reminded one remotely and obscurely of matters clinical and approved, of some sort of reformer or taskmistress rather than of an occultly conspiratorial bedfellow, a decadent but sympathetic courtesan. Not, to be exact, that the latter was the role she wished to play, nor do I think she was fitted for it, her previous experience, in my opinion, being limited to three American marriages and a few Irish gurriers. She had read Lawrence, and for her sex was not a matter of febrile and delectable deviations from the straight and narrow, but a wide road to a good healthy bash. She was accustomed to say, "fuck", as I fucked, this on Lawrentian grounds, and with all due respect to progressive opinion, I can only say it put me off.

In short, if not exactly an expense of spirit in a waste of shame, Eunice was certainly often an expense of energy for what was not always a sufficient reward. Why then did I continue the association? Well, the reader will already have gathered that I am a fairly malleable sort of person. Also, in the early days, in the accursed weakness of the moment, I had made certain protestations from which I now found it difficult to disassociate myself. It is a vice from which I have never been free, and at a later part of this history I may have occasion to tell of what dire complications, in another relationship, it caused. But in Eunice's case also circumstances were against disengagement, for she had the entrée to Sir Mortlake's almost nightly parties—as who had not?—and if I did not visit her often enough at her flat she could always come to The Warrens and trap me beside the New World Bible and the odd socks. Thirdly, and perhaps most important, let me make no bones about it, I was the victim of propaganda, not hers alone but a vast system of persuasion difficult to resist. As a result of this propaganda I felt that a certain, not so much public, as private prestige attached to the relationship; whereas, of course, as a result of the same propaganda, I felt that nothing but disgrace attached to my relationship with Bridget. That I was often forced to enjoy Eunice in the image of Bridget, thus allying the three of us in a curious metaphysical bond, from which, alas, only I and Eunice were the gainers, and Eunice perhaps most of all, did little I am afraid to diminish such satisfaction as I got from obeying the behests of the propaganda in question.

Fortunately Eunice much preferred progressive, poetic evenings in Baggot Street to my cubby hole in Sir Mortlake's. Once the field had narrowed down more or less to me, she became somewhat choosy about going there, and her buttered American accents were heard less often underground, lifted in the strains of "Jo Hill" and other leftery-folkery Americana. When she did come, she would attempt to prevail on me to return to her flat. It was nearly always three or four o'clock before the Warrens broke up and I would seldom move until the drink was gone. The result was that my slumbers on these occasions were altogether insufficient. Besides, if one has to go out working in the morning it is always better to wake up in the accustomed place, and to go through the motions like an old horse being woken in its stable. An unaccustomed vista somehow increases the horror of hurrying, late as usual, through the rain or the sleet.

What Eunice most preferred however were quiet evenings under the pink lamp with the poems of John Donne, and, I will claim this for her, a bottle of Jameson, to be followed, when the poetry had been duly appreciated, by stretching exercises between the pink sheets. From these improving encounters I would usually endeavour to escape before the last bottle of stout was consumed or thrown in The Warrens, for I liked a little relaxed company after them, and I preferred to wake up on my own palliasse and to be free to think a little of Bridget before I fell asleep. As things settled down we arrived at a tacit understanding that I would visit her boudoir one evening or so a week, but on the other evenings I could never be quite sure that she would not hunt me out, either in O'Turk's or later in The Warrens.

It was all a great strain. Between the grocer's committee, Bridget and Eunice, four or more evenings were taken up, some of them in cruel sobriety, and for a man whose nerves were quiet only in the pub this was rather hard. Also, I seldom got to sleep before four o'clock, what with Sir Mortlake's parties, or Eunice, or both together. Further, between Bridget and Eunice and my public and my private lives, I was beginning to resemble one of those unfortunate animals which are driven potty by being exposed to a series of contradictory stimuli, so that the one which previously meant food now means an electric shock, a nervous crisis being brought on by flashing the lights out of sequence when the poor rat is just getting the hang of it.

So, in a way, my man the Secretary had a point when he suggested that my extra-mural activities might be having a detrimental effect on my abilities. Unrewarding though they might be, the very shortage of sleep alone rendered proper attention to the mysteries of the Granulated Sugar Distribution of In Accordance with Pre-War Requirements, Emergency Powers Order Number 155A, almost impossible. Nor was one's will to work noticeably improved by the sight of three or four former major-generals, a warned-off solicitor and an unpublished Marxist poet comfortably disposed in various corners of the great kitchen, at least able to sleep off the hang-over, probably able to get through the day with a sufficiency of drink and a modicum of food, as one staggered breakfastless and ill at the evil hour of nine o'clock to a place of pain, disgrace and shame beyond measure, for no motive that could be discerned (since for most of the week I was as broke as they were) except some spurious morality which probably cloaked a lack of trust in God's providence.

One Sunday morning, after such a gathering in The Warrens, I helped Sir Mortlake collect the empties and transport them to the pub. It was a fair haul, about ten dozen and worth a pound, but the baronet, though he had a good heart, was not notorious for his readiness to buy, so there was a noticeable pause before the ordering of the first drink. Though it was only Sunday, and the grocers paid me on Thursday, I of course had nothing.

"It seems to me, my dear," said Sir Mortlake, reluctantly disbursing the price of two Guinness, "that you get the worst of both worlds. You slave away all day and every day, morning, noon and night in the cause of grocing, and yet you never seem to have a penny."

We gazed around the pub. Perhaps half of those present had no visible means of support. All appeared to be quietly enjoying themselves.

"Personally I think you'd be much better off if you abandoned the grocing entirely. I'm sure the poor dears have got lots of terrible problems on their hands and need you most desperately, and I'm sure you're a tremendous help to whatever it is you're supposed to be assisting, but unless you feel you've got a real vocation for it I shouldn't be surprised if you didn't find yourself happier just sitting in the pub like these gentlemen." He gestured towards a group which included an ex-coalheaver who had once read Kropotkin and never gone short of a drink from that day forward, a former egg-inspector who had an enormous repertoire of arcane and tuneless Irish ballads and was consequently much in demand among the limeys, and a farm labourer who had had his ear bitten off by a policeman in a fight outside a Thomas Street shebeen.

"But Morty," I said, "I haven't got a revolutionary past."

"That's absolutely no reason, my dear, why you shouldn't have a revolutionary present. Much better in my opinion. You give up your big job with these wicked capitalists. . . ."

"Small tradesmen, Morty."

"Capitalists is much better. Anyway you give up your big job because you have read Spengels or whatever he was called, and Bob, as you might say, is your flipping uncle. I could never quite master the jargon myself, but you have a talent for that sort of thing. Heaven knows, if they can support that"—he gestured towards the one-eared subversive—"they can support you. Besides, you're a man of letters. You spend most of the week in a state of destitution anyway. The grocing impedes your drinking and vice versa. You sit here, my dear, composing your little poems and speaking harshly of society, and even if you don't do any better you can't very well do worse. I know I should advise you otherwise, because I've got my rent to think of, but I have every confidence in your ability to raise such a trifling sum and in my funny old way I have got your interests at heart. Besides you know, you could have the broom cupboard for ten bob a week, at least until you find your feet,

To tell you the truth I've had an offer of five bob more than you're paying for the wine cellar. Think it over, my dear."

And benignly he bought me another Guinness.

THE grocers' committee met on Monday nights. This particular Monday they were all in fine fettle, having just accomplished the ruin of some wretched price-cutter. The large Players circulated merrily, some of them in my direction. The Chairman made his usual witticism, and this time everybody smiled as if we all shared a joke.

"Do any good at Leopardstown, Meehaul?"

"O divil the bit. They're sometimes very hard to find."

"They are indeed. They are indeed. I had the last though. The wife's cousin is married to Doherty's sister and I can tell you they were very confident. It won in a canter too. They know what they're doing that crowd. It's seldom they make a mistake. There's damn few flies on them. I often hear a bit from that direction. Pity I didn't see you before the last and I could have tipped you the wink."

"Well, to tell you the truth, at that stage, Bill, I don't think I would have taken any man's word for anything, even yours. It wasn't a shortage of information I was suffering from, I can tell you, but the reverse. If I had stuck to the book of form, as in my own quiet way I usually do, I would have been a wiser and richer man. Not, of course, that I ever have much on. It's a day in the open air, that's the way I principally look on it. By the way, Maurice, I don't know whether you've seen a very interesting series of articles in *The Philanthropist* about the necessary diminishment in efficiency of the retail combine in proportion to its size. Theoretical, of course, but there are one or two things of interest. I've kept them in case you hadn't seen them. Perhaps you might like to read them and pass them on. Of course as you'll spot yourself immediately it's simply the old law of diminishing returns looked at from the consumer standpoint—regarding all retail distribution as in fact an investment on the part of the consumer, an idea as you know better than anyone that's not new to us here."

"Faith, Meehaul, I wish it was the consumer that lost his money when some hard-working family grocer's driven out of business, hah hah, heh?"

"Hah hah. Well of course that's a way of looking at it too, Joe. But the point Maurice and myself and this clever fellow in *The Philanthropist* are making, is that it really is in the end. The customer stands to lose in the heel of the hunt, though he may not know it when he's swapping his stamps or his coupons for his Japanese camera. Well, gentlemen, shall we get to business?"

And all went merry as a marriage bell. A long-standing dispute with the bacon curers had been resolved to everybody's satisfaction. The process by which the unfortunate price-cutter had been driven out of business received an official gloss. The dismaying loss of membership in the mountain fastnesses of the south-west had been discovered by the Secretary's acumen to be due to the malefactions of a local organiser. The Secretary was able to report that this individual was now, happily, in gaol, and that membership figures on those remote frontiers had taken a turn for the better. There was a palpable atmosphere of mutual congratulation all round, in which even I shared. Gazing at the happy faces, I felt the thrill of belonging. Silently collating all this good news in my large notebook prior to incorporating it in the minutes, I was possessed by the spirit of efficiency and service and good grocing. Oh, it was cosy there in that lighted, smoke-filled room, in that silent building, in that deserted street. We were all in concord and we all, even I, belonged. I thought it over again.

COME Tuesday morning things wore a different aspect. It was autumn, and equinoctial cloud held Dublin in thrall. When the broken alarm clock went off on the floor I could sense it was raining outside. There had been an unusually large and boisterous gathering in The Warrens the night before. The one-eared subversive was asleep in a corner of the kitchen. I discovered I had no bus-fare. It took a long time to wake him, perhaps because of the impediment to his hearing, and before I had secured my sixpence, an English lady painter who had arrived in Ireland on a brief visit some weeks previously, appeared from an inner chamber where she had spent the night with two revolutionary major-generals. She was already, even at that hour of the morning, back in the full spate of enthusiasm about the Irish character that had carried her to double seduction the night before. My difficulties being explained, she produced a ten bob note from a hand-worked leather purse. Minimal gratitude demanded perfunctory agreement with, and development of, her remarks about the natives and their charms, so that it was almost ten o'clock when I arrived, breakfastless, hung-over, dirty and wet, at the office; now stripped, as in the aftermath of some fairy banquet, of the feeling of light and security that had invested it the night before.

My man the Secretary arrived unusually early and more than usually louring of brow. I allowed the regulation ten minutes to elapse and then I entered with the letters. The scowl that met me was like a physical barrier to my advance across the room. I began to explain what I thought the first letter was about, but he waved my maunderings aside with a gesture which indicated the magnitude of his restraint as well as the illimitable depths of his contempt.

"Are you aware . . ." he began, and paused. "No, I don't suppose you are. The Chairman rang up here at nine forty-five this morning. AT A QUARTER TO TEN."

"Oh," I said. "They didn't tell me."

"They weren't here. Do you understand that? They weren't here. There was nobody here. Not one single, solitary, member of the staff of this organisation. The place was deserted. AT A QUARTER TO TEN."

"Oh."

"You may well say oh, and double oh. And do you know what the Chairman did then?"

Of course I did not, but shook my head, assuming as best I could an expression in which were combined, polite enquiry, breathless anxiety, and deep contrition. God knows, hung-over as I was, I felt all three.

"The Chairman rang me up at my home. At ten minutes to ten. And do you know what the Chairman said?"

The question was again ridiculous, but I went through the same pantomime.

"'Where,' he said, 'is your staff? Is there an outing to Bray with a picnic and a melodeon, or has there been a strike. Have they all,' he said, 'dropped dead? Or have they all got German measles or mumps? I thought Riley was looking a bit greener around the gills than usual last night,' he said, 'and of course he was up very late at that committee meeting. You shouldn't work him too hard,' he said, 'he's a delicate class of a fellow.'"

I wondered whether a smile was indicated and decided not to risk it.

"Well?"

"My clock didn't go off," I said.

"And I suppose everybody else's clock was similarly afflicted? It must be radiation. If I've told you once I've told you a hundred times that if you're not on time those women will not be on time. I've begged you on my bended knees to get here at the proper hour in the morning. I've gone out of my way to give you the advice of an older man and a man with experience. This is not a charitable institution. We—you and I—we are merely employees, employed to do a job of work and to do it properly, that is to say to the satisfaction of our employers. I, even I, am merely the servant of my committee. Nothing more. Do you understand that? And now what happens? The Chairman rings me up. At ten minutes to ten. To say there is not a sinner in the office. Not a solitary sinner. In other words I cannot delegate the simplest function to you. I cannot trust you to undertake even the most elementary responsibility?"

He paused. Fury had given way to a sort of dull stare. I had nothing to say, except perhaps to agree with him on this last point, which I felt would have been wrong.

"Do you know what I was doing this morning? I suppose you think I was lying in bed. I have been up since half-past seven preparing our evidence for the butter commission, and then, at ten minutes to ten I learn, on the telephone, from the Chairman's own lips . . ."

Words failed him. He picked up the first letter. I

expected a stormy session with them, but I was wrong. He was subdued, matter of fact, patient, explanatory.

When they had all been either retained or returned he asked, as he frequently did, "Is there anything else?"

"Yes," I said, "there is. I shall be leaving pretty soon."

He was impatient and puzzled. "You'll be what?"

"Leaving. I mean I would like to give notice."

"You'd like to give notice. And what, might I ask, do you intend to do?"

"Well," I said, "I was thinking of begging in the pub for a while."

"Of what?"

"Of begging in the pub."

"Well. I see. Well, begod, the hours might suit you better anyway. They don't open so early. I don't suppose you'll want a reference for that?"

"No, no, I don't think I'll want a reference. You never know, but I think my business career is probably over."

"I suppose you realise that I haven't had my summer holidays yet? You've forgotten I put them off because of the messenger boys' strike and the bacon commission and the mixed trading act, to say nothing of the Corporation market plan?"

"No, no."

"I suppose it doesn't matter anything to you whatever. I had rather planned on having a break towards the end of the month."

"Well, would you like me to stay on for a little while longer?"

"Oh no. Not if you've made hard and fast arrangements with the, eh, clientele of the pub. To say nothing of the management. I'm sure it would be a great disappointment to them too. And I don't suppose a successor will be too difficult to find. Do you expect, might I ask, to better yourself by the beggary? Or is it a vocation pure and simple?"

"Well, if it comes to that, it wouldn't be too hard, would it?"

"If I can be of any assistance to you, be sure and let me know, and if it turns out you need a reference for a police permit or anything like that, of course I'll give you a reference all right, don't worry. As soon as you've made final arrangements you might tell us the name of the pub so that we can drop in every now and then and put something in the hat. I'm sure the chairman would be only too delighted, being a great admirer of yours, as you are doubtless aware."

I HAVE already given the reader a general outline of the sorts and conditions of beggary obtaining in that particular milieu, at that particular time. I moved into the broom cupboard, a cosy but cramped apartment under the bricked-off stairs to the upper world. It did not quite accommodate the length of a mattress, so that one slept in a hollow and it was impossible to stretch out fully, but there was room beside the mattress for the dirty socks and the New World Bible and an empty bottle or two. The alarm clock I no longer needed.

My life changed dramatically for the better. The immense privilege, enjoyed only by a tiny minority, either of the rich or the poor, of lying on in the mornings, was restored to me. My worries vanished, and were replaced by mere problems. I could snatch at the passing moment, unencumbered by the necessity to return to a place of business and exploit every stroke of luck, a visiting American, an amusing acquaintance, a coterie of drunks, that the days in their infinite variations might provide. The advantages of this were enormous, and my technique of beggary, already practised perforce on a part-time basis, improved out of all recognition now that I had time and professional status. I ate sporadically it is true, but with more appetite and leisure. My acquaintance burgeoned and I drank with no eye on the clock except that consciousness of time made necessary by the laws of the land. It is true that Bridget—as my clothes deteriorated, and my gait became a shambles due to the worsening condition of my shoes, and I was even more frequently than before compelled to request her to pay for this and that—became rapidly and openly unsympathetic. The weather had broken, the parks and open spaces were impossible, and most of our private converse took place in doorways, flanked by other murmuring doorways, round about the hostel.

"I want to go in," she would say. "It's late already. Let me go, Paddy. And listen, by the way, you should get your hair cut. You're a holy show. Oh stop that, Paddy. Indeed then I will not. To that dreadful place? And for what? For no good reason I'm sure."

Then she would turn the sporadic conversation cagily, in her genuinely ingenuous way, round to the question of the job. Some of her acquaintance had seen me shambling down Grafton Street once or twice during office hours and her suspicions were aroused.

"You should take more care of your appearance," she would say tearfully, "if not for my sake then at least for the sake of your job. I don't know what they must think of you at all. Paddy, I asked you to stop it and I mean it."

Then she would yield her lips and, after our poor fashion, her fully clothed body to me, until eventually I would be left with the memory of her profile, angry and sorrowful, as she climbed the steps in the porchlight and let herself in to her vestal abode saying, "I don't know. I may be going out. Anyway I'm on night duty next week. You're altogether impossible."

Finally she began to send her friends to the telephone to say she was out. Then one of them took care to tell me she was out with Doctor O'Rafferty, the House Surgeon. Ultimately she came to the instrument herself to say, after many monosyllables, cross-purposes and pauses, that she had met "a nice boy, and was going out with him very often".

The sweet cheat gone, I mourned a little for the lost contact with her youth and innocence, but the truth was that the interests and preoccupations of my new calling acted, as novelty will, to soften any such blow. Besides, the cardinal principle and cardinal luxury of beggardom is resignation, a state of mind I was determined to enjoy to the full. So the days passed: the long mornings in my hollow, the idle forenoons among the flotsam of the previous night's gathering with cigarettes reconstituted from the butts of the night before, the chances of the afternoon and the evening.

The morning pub, with sweeping and polishing in progress, and the racing page being discussed with calm and authority by all entitled to be present, was a great improvement on the grocers' headquarters at the same hour. Once the initial entrance fee had been paid no one could dispute your right to beg there for the rest of the first session, to accept not only such drink as came one's way, but quietly and confidentially to hold out the hat for hard cash. Not that I needed a great deal of cash in those days, except perhaps to while away the doldrums of the afternoon with a few bets, or to buy a few drinks for myself or impoverished acquaintances during the slack hours. The days were untroubled but not monotonous: the lights coming on in the pub, for it was already winter, about half-past four or five; the influx of released employees, eager to drop the cares of the day, shortly afterwards; the atmosphere of genuine friendship and relaxation that prevailed during those winter evenings while the rain poured down outside, the editor of *Furthest Horizons*, a review to which I sometimes contributed, distributed drinks to selected members of the company by a secret system of signals known only to himself and the barman, and at the whisper of "what'll you have?" in a Japanese or American accent glasses moist from the palm were hurled at the counter from all corners of the establishment.

At closing time, when the rain had lifted and the neon signs were reflected on the wet pavements, the bona fides would be blazing like the coming Christmas on the mountainsides: another fug, another warmth to prove that doom is never final; and the cars would splash out along the mountain roads in an atmosphere of excursion and adventure. Round the bona fide Sir Mortlake would be circulating in the buff waistcoat that had done duty in Mayfair so many suicides ago, suggesting to one and all, without distinction of race, class, creed or employment, that he was giving a little, a *very* little party in The Warrens this evening and he would be so glad if everybody would come and perhaps bring a little, a *very* little to drink. The sugar bags, to the number of perhaps forty or fifty, each holding a round dozen of Guinness, would be loaded into the motorcars; the cavalcade would sweep back to town, and the musty smell of The Warrens would be subsumed for a while in the more festive odour of freshly poured blood. There was never any shortage of motor-cars, bought as they were, and abandoned as they were, on the hire-purchase system.

It seems now to have been a happy time. Perhaps it wasn't. Oddly enough I seem to look back on the hard times, and there were hard times, with as much nostalgia as for the good: rainy afternoons in my broom cupboard when the pubs had proved an absolute blank, with the socks and the bottles and the New World Bible.

I am not, as the reader will perhaps have gathered (and if I may venture for once on a little self-characterisation) easily afflicted or cast down by what is called sordidity. Like Doctor Johnson, I have no great passion for clean linen. I have stood in company with my unseen garments—socks, underpants, vest—representing the elemental facts of existence, and felt, if anything, comforted by their reminder. There is a definite sense in which a mere palliasse, let us say my u-shaped mattress, in a corner, let us say my broom cupboard, covered by a single . . . not dirty, dirty is not the word, nor is unwashed . . . by a single permanent blanket, is a home not only for man's body but for his soul, whereas the sterilities of suburbia are homes for nothing.

About this aspect of my life I felt that the gentlemen whose opinions were collected in the New World Bible would sympathise and understand. And as my condition worsened I was to discover that given a certain frankness of approach, women, in truth and in private, did also. Their preference for the elemental facts of existence could eventually be elicited. Not that I smell. Far from it. I do not seem to have the metabolism.

One of the snags about beggary, however, is that it is difficult to draw the line between a readiness to oblige in small matters in return for gifts and presents, and outright employment, often of a most degrading kind. This is particularly so with the beggar in the role of guest, and by the nature of their calling beggars are more frequently to be found in the role of guest than other mortals.

Being a successful guest involves a definite change of status, with a different set of rules, which must be watched and observed. Comfort apart, there is all the difference in the world between being offered money for a night's lodging and being offered the lodging itself. The latter having transpired, it is essential to remember that you take rank with the Prime Minister of the United Kingdom enjoying a fortnight's shooting with the Duke of Rockerbottom. And even though you outstay your welcome, be it more or less, there are decencies to be observed up to the last moment. "You must go on Friday" means, after all, "you can stay till Friday". "You must buy your own food" means when all is said and done, "you can continue to use my bed, or my mattress, or my floor, or sleep in the bath". Yet such are the snags attached to guesthood that in my opinion it can be much more demoralising than outright beggary. I do not mean that either are specially or necessarily demoralising—much less so than sitting there, with my back to his door, assisting the secretary for example—but in so far as there is demoralisation attached to either, as there is, let's face it, to practically everything, the guests have it. I do not wish to run ahead of my story, but there is no doubt that over-prolonged guesthood induces a certain timidity in a man, the principal symptoms being the light cough, the springy walk, the first thing in the morning smile and the smile on entering, and a variant of locomotor ataxis, brought on by constant anticipation of the host's wishes, which manifests itself in a hoppiness of movement, a birdlike cocking of the head at the slightest provocation, a kind of St. Vitus' dance which cannot be stilled even when the sufferer is pretending to be immersed in his book.

There is also, to go back to my original point, the danger, ever present when one is depressed in spirit, of being manoeuvred from the position of guest into that of dependent servant, so that one wakes up in the morning and finds one has a job, has perhaps had a job for some weeks, and a damned ill-paid job at that. It is all too easy to decline from being generally obliging, doing the washing up, stepping down the road for a newspaper or a packet of fags, slapping a coat of paint on that shed, or baby-sitting and suchlike, to becoming a general handyman, hopping and hod-carrying from pillar to post, remonstrated with and abused in a way no properly employed servant would stand, on the job at all hours of day and night like a Victorian slavey, and miles from base maybe and therefore to all intents and purposes an actual chattel-slave until a begging-letter bears fruit and secures one's manumission in the form of the journey-money. A simple readiness to oblige is proper and natural enough when one is taking advantage of another man's possessions; indeed if he does go out to work it is only right to help him in every way one can consistent with one's freedom to sleep and meditate; but it is a quick and slippery slope from friendly helper to actual bond-serf, abused for one's laziness and derided for one's incompetence.

In this situation as in so many others, as in beggary itself, or assisting a secretary, or a hundred and one other things, it is essential to remember that demoralisation is progressive, and that a thoroughly demoralised man is of no use to himself or anyone else. Once demoralisation sets in both parties get the worst of the bargain. Instead of a witty and amusing guest, the host finds he has an unbelievably incompetent and abjectly terrified idiot around the house; instead of an erudite, lightheartedly malicious, fanciful and perhaps poetic drinking companion, the steamer finds that the man he is forking out for is a morose but servile moron who knocks over the drink in his anxiety to furnish the match.

You have to watch each downward step, and since successful beggary depends so greatly on the status of the beggar, it is essential to maintain a reserve of decorum, amounting at times to stand-offishness. I had status enough, of a kind, in those days. After all, had I not just abandoned a job, retired—to use the secretary's phrase—from public life? It was not difficult to suggest I had done so out of left-wing anarchical principle. I could parade my disgust with the affairs of state with a knowledge which few aspirants to the crown of martyr could muster. I did not need to adopt an exiguous left-wing philosophy to be regarded with sympathy and admiration by the wearers of turtle-necked sweaters. The New World Bible was anarchic enough, and the anarchy it suggested combined suitably with the vague hints of messianic devotion to art I threw out; for I did not scruple to throw also, though delicately it is true, and with some misgivings, my dedication to art into the pot. I did not of course quote the religious masters of Asia and the Levant directly. The debt I owe to them for those days is rather that they provided me with a mood, a nexus round which an attitude could coagulate, an attitude suitably vague but thoroughly angry, an attitude of revolt tinged with despair, which allowed me, let me say it, to trade on my dedications without actually mentioning them, an attitude which legalised the role of beggary and conferred upon it at the same time an almost intimidating status. After all, had not many of the gentlemen whose words the compilers of the New World Bible saw fit to perpetuate been beggars themselves?

My acquaintance at this time was as previously described, and I believe I have said something about that element in it which was heavily biased towards art and left-wingery, often English or Anglo-Irish, frequently in possession of a little cash, Sir George Dermot, I suppose, belonged to this element, but quite distinctively. I first became acquainted with him, in O'Turk's, coming up to the Yuletide season, on a bitterly cold day when a pall of snow-clouds lay over the city and the lights in the pub were on all day. It must not be supposed that I regarded everybody I met with what is called a professional eye. No, no, far from it. If I have given that impression I have done wrong. My beggary was simply and literally the absence of a profession, in no sense a profession in itself. Apart from anything else, this conferred status on me. Many of my fellow beggars were not thus distinguished.

Sir George was a huge, passionate but cherubic person, rather like a middle-aged, Anglo-Irish, Botticelli infant. He lived, I was to discover, in an ancestral castle deep in the mountains, a gaunt fastness amid a barren but beautiful waste, a waste of deep continually changing colours and extraordinary light-effects. I say I was to discover, for when we drove out there, as we did, in a sort of possessed jeep, the snow was falling out of black darkness and we galloped over roads on which it was already an inch or so thick. We had a couple of quick bracers in the last threatened outposts of the bona fide belt before tackling the mountain passes. Sir George was in fine fettle, plunging and snorting upward into the darkness.

"Monstrous," he declared. "Monstrous, how the world is run. No place for art, no place for beauty, no place for Jews, no place for negroes. No place for you except that awful job. No place for me. Is it any wonder"—he reached swiftly behind the seat, extracted a bottle of whiskey from the darkness, uncorked it with his teeth, drank off a liberal measure, then passed it to me—"is it any wonder that I live out here in the mountains with my sweetie pie and these simple, these unspoilt, these beautiful people, in this beautiful, this unspoilt, this primitive place, is it any wonder that I have to get back, that I cannot bear it, cannot bear it. . . ."

His sobs were drowned by the howling of the engine and the howling of the wind. Great globules of good Irish whiskey were pouring down his cheeks. Grief and fury possessed him.

"We must get back," he shouted, "we must get back to Ardash. You must come with me. I can promise you nothing but peace. Adeline will love you, and you can walk and you can read and you can think and you can forget. Forget the monstrous, monstrous people that hate humanity and hate art and . . . and all the rest of it. I can promise you nothing but peace. But you must come, you must come to my house, to my home and forget all these monstrous people."

Lacerated by rage and sorrow he grabbed my arm while the car cavorted wildly across the road. In the dashboard light his cherubic face was transformed into teeth and fury.

He was tending to repeat himself, for this was the invitation that I had been given in identical terms in the pub. It should by now have been obvious that I was going, indeed it was beginning to be plain that no power in heaven or on earth could any longer intervene to save me.

The road curved abruptly leftward.

"I can't wait, I can't wait," cried Sir George, the whiskey streaming down his cheeks. "We must get back. We must get back. Bloody road goes the long way round. Shorter"—he gestured with his right arm—"shorter across the top."

He pulled the jeep to the left, gnashed into a lower gear, hauled it to the right and put it at the wall. There was a clatter of stones as we went over, sailing through the darkness while the engine and Sir George roared together, one tremendous bump on the other side and then we were off across the heather.

"Damn clever invention," conceded Sir George to the outside world. "Four wheel drive, six forward gears, strong as a bull, jumps like a stag."

I did not altogether share his confidence in the machine, yet the sensation of bouncing through the black, snow-filled void was not altogether unpleasant, like exploring a new element.

"Don't worry, old chap," cried Sir George, above the furies. "Often go this way. Not the slightest risk. Got to get back, to Adeline, and peace, and music, and love. Only one sticky patch, but there's a good stiff frost tonight and the bog won't bother us. You love music"—I didn't, but I let it pass—"you love music. They hate it, just as they hate you and me and Jews and negroes and these simple unspoilt people and art and poetry and all the rest of it. Do you know Mahler's 'Song of the Earth'? We'll play it tonight. Wonderful music, wonderful."

As if in response to the mention of the "Song of the Earth", the vehicle began to sink. Screaming with pain and frustration, all four wheels rotating, it splashed snow and bog-water into the darkness. At length Sir George desisted.

"I'm afraid we can't go any further," he announced. "I was a bit rash, ha, ha, ha." His laughter overcame him. Tears deluging his cheeks, he offered me the bottle. Then he was suddenly serious again. "It's lovely having you to stay with us, dear fellow, lovely. A little civilisation in this awful, terrible, monstrous, outrageous world, a little enclave of peace and love and music and painting and poetry."

I reflected that we were in the middle of a bog, somewhere on a mountainside, in a snow-storm and impenetrable darkness, but I held my peace.

"This bloody awful idiotic thing is still sinking," said Sir George. "We'd better take the other five bottles of whiskey and get out. There's a tenant of mine lives somewhere down there. An ignorant ass, absolutely under the thumb of the parish priest, deluded fellow, very superstitious, monstrous the influence of the clergy in this country, absolutely monstrous, this fellow's very primitive, priest is an absolute tyrant, worse than Hitler, far worse, still we'll knock the old fellow up, he'll have an ass and cart or something, we'll have to go back to the road, can't do this bit on foot. Here, you put these two in your pockets. Dear old chap."

We struggled painfully and wetly out of the bog and set off across the mountainside, Sir George entertaining me as we went with a full account of Captain Scott's tragic expedition to the South Pole, frequently stopping in the falling snow and freezing wind to act out particular episodes, such as the breakdown of the tractors, or the death of Captain Oates.

WE arrived at Ardash in the small hours, on a donkey cart driven by the superstitious peasant, who had in fact turned out to be a man of the utmost liberalism, tolerance and good humour. ("Charming old fellow," said Sir George to me. "Absolutely unspoilt, wonderful sense of humour, one of nature's gentlemen, civilisation as old as the stone-age, pagan really.") Now with Sir George wearing the old man's Sunday trousers and myself his "workin' wans", the donkey cart wound through the snow under the demesne walls of Ardash Castle, through the battered gateposts and up the gloomy drive between the trees.

We traversed the empty entrance-hall, followed a flagged passageway on the left, descended a short flight of steps and paused before a door, from behind which came the sound of revelry. An old and quavering voice was raised in song: "Oft in the stilly night, ere slumber's chains have bo-ound me . . ." "Uncle Apsey," said Sir George, "bloody old fool" and thrust open the door.

There were half a dozen people seated round the kitchen table, including two coal-black negroes, man and woman, in flowing robes. The singer, a white-moustached old gentleman, abruptly sat down.

"Adeline," cried Sir George, "I have brought you a friend. I have brought him home, home to my sweetie-pie, and peace, and love, and music."

Is it the imagination of memory, or at the mention of

the word music did a shadow pass over the faces of the assembled company, even the black ones, even, now that I think of it, the face of the woman who rose to greet me? Tall, with her long black hair loose to her shoulders, Lady Adeline resembled the Mona Lisa, even to the touch of sluttishness in that lady and the vaguely drunken, secretive smile.

"Welcome," she said, blowing ash from the cigarette between her lips. "Welcome home. By the way, what's your name?"

"He is a poet," said Sir George, "a great poet. He has just resigned a job as chairman of a grocery or a distillery or something because he couldn't stand it any longer, couldn't stand those awful, monstrous people who hate us all, and he has come here for peace, and love, and music."

This time there was no mistaking it. The word produced a tremor that communicated itself from member to member of the company.

"Let me introduce you all, dear sweet people. And let's have another drink. Come in, Connors, come in," he called into the passageway, where the old man stood smiling in the shadows.

I am not clever at picking up introductions, but I gathered that the negro's name appeared to be Obe Jasus and that "these good sweet, gentle, innocent people are here to help me with my potting, which even with these people here is so neglected, my poor sweet, gentle potting."

For the next two hours or so all went as mellowly as the whiskey. Sir George reminisced and the company relaxed. There were, for the time being, no further references to the sinister music. We heard, among other things, the story of how Sir George had once pursued a well-known English art-critic who was staying at Ardash through the woods with a poker, and how the wretched fellow had eventually escaped by climbing a tree which resisted Sir George's bulk. There he had remained, treed fast, until his pitiful cries were heard towards dawn by a Civic Guard out after poteen, who had prevailed upon Sir George to " let the poor man go about his business, whatever it is, and don't you be minding his opinions about your friend MacTeese at all ".

As the evening progressed, I learned something about the rest of the company, and was to gather more before my stay at Ardash came to a close. There were two or three distant cousins of Sir George's, all maintained patriarchally at Sir George's expense. There was Uncle Aspey, who had had a mysterious career, partly it seemed in the British army and partly in the British Foreign Office, and a mysterious disgrace, shrouded and far back in time, but involving probably a prison sentence of some duration and certainly some loss of spirit. Uncle Apsey did the cooking and did it, when sober, surprisingly well. He looked like a Buchan general gone wrong, and in a perpetual state of vague fear. There were Obe Jasus and his wife, Nigerian intellectuals who had been recruited, ostensibly to help Sir George with the " pottery ", through one of the recognised conduits of the slave traffic, the advertising columns of *The New Statesman*, one of those advertisements, you know the kind, promising plenty of leisure for student or artist in return for light duties, pocket money only we're afraid, but plenty of wholesome food and good conversation in beautiful part of the world. All of this advertisement was undoubtedly true—Sir George was undoubtedly a man of honour—but it did not state the whole truth, which in any case would have been unbelievable and occupied several columns of *The New Statesman*, supposing that progressive organ had consented to print it, which is doubtful, to say the least.

There followed various further tales of violent vengeance on the philistine before, turning to Lady Adeline with tears in his eyes, Sir George declared, "It's wonderful having this young man here with us honey-dovey, though we can offer him nothing, nothing at all but a little peace."

He turned to me. "Nothing, do you hear me, absolutely nothing but peace and love and music. It's monstrous, but we have nothing to give you, nothing. I have nothing left. They have taken it all away from me. If I were rich you would never have to go back into that terrible job again, that terrible job in the distillery that you hate and that you will have to go back to because there is no place at all for people like us, for artists or Jews or negroes."

Then he glared suddenly on the company and crying, "Come, my friends, my dear friends, let us crown this wonderful evening by going to the music-room and listening to some music," he stood up from his chair.

There followed, I could see, a conflict of wills, deep, silent and terrible, in which the principle protagonists appeared to be Sir George and Obe Jasus, the other members of the company preserving a shifty silence, but glancing, now towards Sir George, now towards Obe Jasus, as if in wild but secret hopes of a surprise outcome. Sir George won. We adjourned, bottles and glasses in hand, to the music-room, where all of us, the elderly and now quite drunken peasant included, sat before a turf-fire while Sir George played, record by record, Mahler's masterpiece.

Dominated by an excessively large gramophone, and with walls lined with shelves of gramophone records, the music-room was, as I later discovered, after the kitchen, the principal room of the establishment, though not in truth, on an ordinary democratic vote for vote basis, the best loved.

The gramophone was of the old-fashioned winding kind, since the electricity generating system, invented, but not quite successfully dominated, by Sir George, was neither reliable nor suitable. The horn of this gramophone was colossal, vastly larger than the one that appears, in touching circumstances, on the label of a well-known manufacturer, in fact it could have accommodated several dogs' noses at once and projected a good five or six feet from the machine itself into the centre of the room. It was awe-inspiring, terrifying and inescapable. It produced, to use a word then fashionable, angst.

The " Song of the Earth " is, to my ears at least, a comparatively noisy work, yet after a time, there began to be apparent above it a persistent snoring noise. On the hearth rug in front of the fire there slumbered an immense Labrador dog and beside him, also slumbering, lay Uncle Apsey. Beyond him again, propped against the turf basket, eyes now peacefully closed, though whether in rapture or in sleep it was hard to say, was the ancient Connors. Sir George himself lay sprawled in an armchair, and his eyes too were closed, though certainly not in sleep, for as each record ended he sprang to his feet to replace it and re-wind the gramophone, accompanying the action each time with enthusiastic comment. Once when he had just performed this ceremony, the music and the snoring rose to a dreadful crescendo together. His eyes still closed, Sir George cried out sharply: " Will nobody put that old thing outside? " One of the distant cousins, who had been poised, whiskey glass in hand, on the edge of his chair, looked at the three elderly sleepers in an agony of indecision. Without opening his eyes, Sir George cried out again, more sharply, "Put that old thing outside, I tell you."

The cousin, possibly confused by the music, hesitated a moment, then as Sir George stirred impatiently in his chair, he opted for Uncle Apsey. With some difficulty, as the old man protested in his drunken sleep, he succeeded in dragging him across the carpet and through the door. We heard a murmuring outside and then the cousin returned to his seat. The snoring continued.

Sir George opened his eyes.

"Connors, you're snoring," he shouted. "Wake up and listen to the music."

"Indeed then I am not, sir," said Connors, sitting bolt upright on the floor immediately. "I haven't had a wink of sleep since yourself and your friend here arrived at my house out of the snow and put on my Sunday trousers."

"Shut up and listen, Connors," said Sir George. "Have you no sense of music?"

"And I take it hard you should malign me like that too, sir," continued the old man, "for there's no wan likes a bar of a song with a glass of malt better than I do. I remember when I was a young fellow I could render a bar of a song as well as that divil that's singin' now in whativir language . . ."

"For the love of God, Connors, will you shut your gab and listen to the beautiful music," roared Sir George.

He leaned back in his chair and closed his eyes once more in rapture. Temporarily suspended, the snoring began again. Sir George opened his eyes. He glared in a fury round the room. The dog growled and twitched. "The Song of the Earth" was evidently inducing nightmares. Everybody looked straight ahead. The music had not had so overtly attentive an audience since it had begun. Sir George glared at his cousin. "I thought," he demanded, in a voice low with rage, "I told you to put that old thing outside?"

The cousin dragged the ancient, still sleeping animal to the door. Outside it Uncle Aspey could be heard, plaintively but persistently protesting. The cousin tip-toed back in. One eye on Sir George, he collected Uncle Apsey's glass and tip-toed out again. Connors' innocent old blue eyes gleamed victoriously. As the cousin resumed his seat the record came to an end. Sir George paused before re-winding the gramophone.

"Monstrous," he cried, achieving more volume even than the machine. "That we, even we, here, in this oasis, this pool, this cesspond, of peace and love, cannot listen to this beautiful, this magnificent music without, without . . ." Words failed him. "As for you Connors," he cried, "you can take your donkey and cart and your Sunday trousers and go home any time you like. Take anything, take everything that's in my house. Take my whiskey, take anything you like, but let me listen to the monstrous music."

"Begob sir," said Connors, "as far as I can see there's nobody stoppin' you at all except yourself. And as far as the trousers is concerned you're more than welcome to them, aye and to the ould ass and cart as well, for the matter of that. And as for meself, sure I'd rather be here listenin' to the ould songs and havin' a glass of malt than lyin' at home thinkin' of the days that are gone, for it's very hard for an ould man like me to get to sleep sometimes. . . ."

"Will you for Christ's sake shut up, Connors?" bellowed Sir George.

Slowly, stubbornly, Germanically, the "Song of the Earth" swelled to its close.

ARDASH CASTLE was not large as castles, I suppose, go. It stood on the slope of a mountain looking down on its own wood and across a valley at the woods of another mountain, still, for although it was December it had up till now been mild, a rich amalgam of red and gold. Behind it the heather rose to the skyline and it was over the brow and down the slope that Sir George had proposed to descend, taking, as it were, his own castle from the rear.

The interior was comfortable enough, though draughty. There was a flagged, bare entrance hall, remarkable principally for an excessively large painting of a prize ram which had been the pride of Sir George's grandfather's eye, but which he had eventually sold to the then Shah of Persia. There was a room full of books, known as the library, books which spilled off the shelves in wild profusion and on examination proved to be a curious mixture between the original Victorian collection and Sir George's more recent additions dating from the late twenties, with absolutely nothing in between, so that although the works of David Lingstone and Aldous Huxley were both available, the startling contrast between their bindings was not alleviated by the presence of Hall Caine or Annie Besant. There was a kitchen where some sort of patent range perpetually functioned and which was therefore the warmest place in the house. Much of the living of the establishment was in consequence done there.

The mysterious potting took place, or rather did not take place, in what had been the stables, and were now expensively equipped with turntables and kilns. It had once been a hobby of Sir George's. Then he had decided to go into it on a large scale, both to exercise his undoubted artistic talents and to retrieve by a profitable commercial venture his undoubtedly failing fortunes. Somewhere, though, there had occurred one of those mysterious failures of enthusiasm to which we are all subject, and the potting had fallen off, until now Sir George only visited the place in a rage, having received a bank-statement or a bill, to hurl a bottle of whiskey through the door or overturn and attempt to destroy some of the expensive equipment.

It was some months before the final cessation of all pottery that Obe Jasus and his wife had been recruited, to help with the more manual part of the craft, and this theory also explained the presence of the rather depressed, impoverished cousins. Sir George however was at no loss. He had work for all who came, and the nature of this work became apparent to me concurrent with the realisation that I was declining into the status of employee myself: we were all music-listeners.

Night after night, under the lips of the gigantic object in the music-room, Sir George assembled his household and his whiskey, and there we all sat, silent as the grave, the bolder or more energetic or more sycophantic spirits occasionally nodding the head or silently tapping the fingers in the hope that they were in time with the music, the less ambitious slumbering or topping themselves up with malted whiskey, and dreaming of the future or the past.

Uncle Apsey gave me the benefit of his experience.

"I don't mind at all having to listen to the stuff. I never was much of a one for conversation. To tell you the truth I'm a solitary drinker by nature. What I do object to is having to look as if one was at a funeral all the time to signify that one is enjoying it. Sometimes, you know, when I'm sitting there boozing, memories of the old, old days in Budapest or India come back to me, and I find myself, just once in a while, smiling to myself, and, you know, for some odd reason the real mark of concentration on the music is to look as glum as possible, and I've noticed it's quite dangerous to be caught smiling, though obviously a chap can't help feeling cheerful sometimes when he's drinking, now can he? One tip I will give you, and that is make it clear that you always listen to the stuff with your eyes closed. Then if you happen to be having an occasional little snooze nobody will know the difference, see?"

Unfortunately for Uncle Apsey he seemed to suffer from some sort of nervous tick when he was drinking, which caused him not only to smile, but frequently to giggle, and on these occasions Sir George's rage knew no bounds. He would upend the turf-basket over Uncle Apsey's head, or fling him bodily out of the room, or hurl irreplaceable gramophone records at him: indeed it was I believe a secret hope among other members of the establishment that Uncle Apsey's unfortunate weakness would cumulatively deplete Sir George's stock of musical classics to such an extent that the gargantuan machine would have nothing left to feed it.

Another snag was that one had to walk warily where any subject connected with the liberal ethic was concerned, and it was sometimes difficult to keep track of Sir George's precise nuance of opinion. When out of humour with the locals he would describe them as superstitious, priest-ridden, backward, illiterate, god-besotted serfs; and the parish priest was a suspicious, intolerant, bigoted, narrow-minded, fanatical bully. On other occasions they were gentle, unspoiled, dignified, proud, simple children of nature; though it was true that the priest, who had once allegedly cheated Sir George over a carload of turf, rarely got beyond the stage of being 'an amusing rascal'.

"Know them? I should damn well think I do," he would cry. "I've known them since I was in the cradle." (This was not strictly true. Sir George had progressed from the cradle to an English prep and public school, to Oxford, to the Riviera. Only the dreadful aftermath of the war had forced him back to his native land and ancestral home.)

By and large however, although in his actual dealings with his neighbours he treated them as human beings like himself, in conversation, particularly with strangers, theory triumphed and the priest-ridden view of them was the one that prevailed. Indeed to hear Sir George and Lady Adeline, when properly aroused, one would imagine that they themselves were the victims of popular intolerance and clerical bigotry; and that they were constantly hampered in their innocent enjoyments by the prevailing puritanism—the truth of the matter being of course that they could, and did, walk naked on the lawn without arousing more than a pitying incomprehension, not untinged with the affection that the natives reserved for those who were, God help them, not quite right in the head.

Where supposed breaches of the liberal ethic were concerned, pitfalls abounded. Thus on one occasion when an innocent visitor, attempting to share Sir George's indignation about the treatment of a servant by a neighbour, Mrs. Monolough, remarked "Sure you wouldn't do that to any man, barrin' he was a black," he was much surprised to find himself savagely assaulted. Another, who happened to use the phrase "give every man his due" in what seemed to Sir George a suspicious context was similarly beaten. I was never attacked myself, but most members of the household went in constant fear. "I usually push the wardrobe up against the door when I go to bed," said Uncle Apsey. "For some reason I seem to get the brunt of it if he's balked of his original prey."

These peculiarities aside, Sir George was the most generous, and not infrequently the most charming of hosts.

And until the music began to represent a definite threat to my sanity, and listening to it to seem a chore not only difficult and wearisome in itself, but attended by a high mortality rate besides, conditions in Ardash suited me down to the ground. I had been beginning to need a rest from O'Turk's, to say nothing of Eunice. The country air, which I tasted briefly every morning while we hammered down to the pub in the jeep, Obe Jasus's robes floating behind us in the breeze, was doing me good. Sir George, when kept off the liberal ethic, had a delightful store of knowledge about the habits of birds, marine history, mediaeval armoury, life on the Riviera in the early thirties, the merits and demerits of Scotch and Irish and other interesting matters. There were the Victorian authors in the library, succulent poached venison for dinner and unlimited supplies of whiskey.

Still, there was the music, and there was the silence that accompanied the music, when the sins of one's past life rose up before one and danced in procession to its beat. It was like a nightly gaol sentence with a monstrous unstoppable gramophone blaring endlessly into one's defenceless ear. There was the fierce desire to talk, to hold converse, to render, as Connors would have it, a bar or a stave of a song; made more acute by the fact that the compulsory music always began when we were at our liveliest and Sir George in the best of humour. To be transplanted after a sociable and charming winter afternoon in the hospitable kitchen to the dreaded music-room was terrible, whiskey or no; to have to compel the face which all afternoon had been wreathed in smiles to adopt a mask of gloomy concentration for hours on end was almost more than could be borne. One forgot to drink, or fell asleep and contracted dry hangovers in the middle of it, but there was no escape. The worst thing was that I began to dream music: symphonies, oratorios, operas, fugues, sonatas, poured from me night after night until I woke at dawn, haggard with the horror of my own compositions.

It was the music that finally decided me to leave Ardash, pleasant though it was in other respects, but before I left there occurred the incident at Mrs. Monolough's which so nearly resulted in the deaths of her social secretary, Sir George, Obe Jasus and myself. Mrs. Monolough was a near neighbour of Sir George's; that is to say she lived about eight or ten miles away across the heather. She had large social commitments, spent a good part of the year in England and abroad and created quite a splash when she returned to Monolough House. In Ardash Castle she was much disliked. One day in the early Spring, when I had been in regular employment as a music-listener for some months, Sir George proposed that Obe Jasus and I should accompany him to a social function of some kind at Mrs. Monolough's. It was a charitable function, to do, I think, with horses, a beast that Sir George cordially detested, possibly a charity auction or something like that: to this day I am not quite clear. Lady Adeline had flatly refused to go, but Sir George occasionally honoured his obligations as a local dignitary and he seemed anyway in humour for an outing.

The three of us set off after lunch in good heart and fettle, the jeep bounding along under a pale blue sky, the heather glowing in the fragile sunlight, Obe Jasus's handsome face shining with pleasure, Sir George at the top of his anecdotal form. I had a slight suspicion that the day might not end so happily. We stopped twice at village pubs. In the first we were known and passed without remark. In the second, Obe Jasus, who stood six foot two in his Nigerian robes and turban, collected an admiring crowd and was variously described as a witch-doctor and a "sort of a class of a king". We were not, I think, quite sober when we followed a winding drive up the side of a mountain with a stretch of water below us on the left, and came eventually round to the front of Monolough House. This was a much more imposing structure than Ardash and on the lawn in front of it there stood a vast marquee. Thither we decided to repair, surmising rightly that it would contain whiskey.

It was full of tweedy people, several of them known to Sir George, but his mood seemed to have changed; and he replied to salutations with what almost amounted to hostility. There was a bar along one side and there we stood, lowering the yellow malt and looking, to put it mildly, quite out of place: Obe Jasus in his highly coloured robes, Sir George in a duffel coat, myself in my all-purpose cast-offs. We were beginning to be a bit noisy and we were attracting a certain amount of attention, not all of it, I think, friendly.

"Can't think what we've come here for," said Sir George, "can't stand these horrible people. I don't know why we didn't stay at home, in our haven of peace, and love, and friendship, instead of coming here among all these vicious, selfish, monstrous people that hate us, hate you and hate me, hate us all." His brow was lowering and I mentally stood to arms. "I'd better go and pay my respects to the old tartar herself. You stay here and have a drink. She would hate you. She hates me. She hates music."

He left the tent and Obe Jasus and I continued drinking and returning stare for stare, comment for comment on the passers-by. At length a young man in striped trousers, black-jacket, handkerchief, spectacles, and a mirthless but sedulously polite smile came up to us. "May I ask," he said, pleasantly enough, "if you've been invited? This is a private function, you know."

Since neither of us had any very clear idea of the nature of the function, we could only stare back at him impassively, an activity at which Obe Jasus was, when he chose, pretty expert. At length I pointed out that it appeared to be necessary to pay for one's drinks.

"Ah yes, but that doesn't necessarily make the function any less private, does it? Mrs. Monolough is not running a pub."

At this moment Sir George returned.

"These dear, good, kind, sweet, gentle people are friends of mine," he announced, empurpling slightly. "Dear, dear friends. And great artists, who want only peace, and music and sympathy. And why I brought them to this dreadful place, to the house, to the tent of that vicious, selfish woman is more than I can say."

"My dear Sir George," said the young man. "I must ask you not to refer to Mrs. Monolough in that fashion. I am her social secretary. If these people are your friends, that is quite all right."

"It is not all right," said Sir George. "It is by no means all right. You come up to my friends when my back is turned and you insult them." He took in Obe Jasus and myself in a comprehensive gesture. "You hate them because they are Jews and negroes and artists. Because they are superior to you and the dreadful world you inhabit. Because you know they despise you and everything about you, from your horrible soul to your horrible clothes."

At this Sir George took the secretary by the lapels and shook him. The man's life was clearly not worth a moment's purchase. A crowd had gathered and there were cries of alarm. Then a low sound, deep and murmurous, broke upon our ears as the sound of the Zambesi falls must once have broken upon Livingstone's. Obe Jasus was shaking with laughter. It created a diversion. Sir George released the secretary and turned to us with tears in his eyes.

"Can you ever forgive me?" he cried. "Can you ever forgive me for exposing you to the jeers and insults of this horrible mob? I am at fault. I am the one who is to blame. I should never have brought you here among our enemies among these beasts baying for the blood of negroes and Jews and artists. I should never have asked you to degrade yourselves in this fashion." He glared about him terribly, eyes rolling, teeth exposed. For a moment I thought he was going to hurl himself single-handed on the entire assembly. People backed away. "Let us go, my friends, my dear friends," he continued, however. "Let us go home to Adeline, and peace and love, and music."

The secretary was one of those people whose vanity will not permit them to see when the situation is best left alone. "Yes," he said, "I think it would be better if you left, Sir George, and took your friends with you. You will probably see matters in a different light tomorrow."

Sir George was upon him in an instant, but Obe Jasus and I and some of the calmer members of the crowd succeeded in pulling him off before he could grind the glass he had seized from the bar into the unfortunate man's face. We held him for a moment, struggling for words, while the secretary recovered his glasses and mopped whiskey from his eyes and lapels. Then we left, in good order, through a laneway in the crowd.

The jeep was parked on a stretch of gravel at some distance from the marquee. As we climbed in, Obe Jasus and Sir George in front and myself in the back, I caught sight of the secretary man following us somewhat dilatorily across the lawn. His motive, I imagine, was to give the impression that he was escorting us off the premises, and thus give himself some right to claim a victory. I prayed that Sir George would not see him, but it was not to be.

The instant the jeep shot into motion I knew what quarry we were after, and the secretary knew it too. His wild cries for help could be heard above the roar of our accelerating engine as he bounded across the lawn. Fortunately for him Sir George accelerated too fast and for a few seconds the jeep slid sideways, spraying gravel in the air. Then we were on the grass and travelling very fast. For a moment of what must have been agonising indecision the secretary hesitated between the marquee and a broad flight of steps leading up to a terrace that extended along the whole front of the building. He reached the steps with a few seconds to spare and flung himself upwards. I shut my eyes, thinking Sir George was going to tackle the steps as well, but he stopped at their foot and hurled the vehicle into reverse.

"I'll show him," he shouted. "Hold on, dear friends."

We flashed laterally along the lawn in front of the building. A grass bank led up to the terrace, but it was surmounted by a balustrade which would probably have been beyond the jeep's ability. Sir George in any case had a different plan. At the end of the terrace the balustrade came to an end, but the bank continued round the corner.

A leftward sweep to get room for the manoeuvre, a right-about-turn and we had climbed the bank and were on the terrace, bearing down on a crowd of people who had congregated in alarm outside the front doors. Our surprise reappearance created terror and the shock of it betrayed the secretary. Instead of dashing into the building, or hiding himself behind other people's backs (though it is true that neither of those courses might have stopped Sir George) he panicked and ran for it, stooping and screaming, towards the other end of the terrace, while we shot after him through the crowd. When we were only a matter of yards behind, however, he had a moment of good sense, vaulted the balustrade in surprisingly agile fashion and made for the marquee. We were forced to continue to the end where we raced off the terrace at a good sixty miles an hour, bounced once on the sloping bank and then executed far too tight a turn on the grass in time to see the secretary vanish into the tent like a fox going to earth.

The opening he went through was in the middle of one side, away from the house. To point the jeep at it would have necessitated another leftward sweep and right-about-turn on our part, and Sir George's enthusiasm for the chase was impatient of obstacles. Obe Jasus, who had hitherto been sitting straight up, detached and impassive, ducked at the last moment and I cowered down in the back. The jeep tore through the canvas cleanly enough, but what I fancy Sir George forgot was that inside it there would be one of those trestle tables that are used as bars on such occasions. This we instantly struck, hurling it forward in front of us in a great clatter of glass and crockery. Then we struck it again, mounted the wreckage of it and ploughed on into the tent. People scattered in all directions, diving under tables, crawling under the canvas, fighting each other at the exit. I caught a glimpse of the secretary, paralysed and helpless, his mouth open in a silent scream, abandoned and terror stricken in the middle. Fortunately the double impact of the table had caused the jeep to get slightly out of control. It struck one of the poles of the tent, uprooting it and carrying the end forward, struck another almost instantly, cracking it clean across, slewed sideways into the bar at one side, and then, skidding back into the middle, struck the third pole just as we were almost on top of the secretary. The stump of the third pole seemed to catch us underneath and the jeep's wheels rotated ineffectually while the engine roared. Then, silently, majestically, and finally the canvas came down.

For a moment we were in terrible, weighted darkness while the jeep jerked convulsively and the engine screamed. Then Sir George shut it off.

"Are you all right my friends, my dear friends?" he enquired solicitously. We answered in the affirmative. Even Obe Jasus's voice seemed shaken. "Then if you will keep your heads down, I'll try to get this bloody thing out of here. I'll put it into reverse. Very thoughtful fellows, whoever made it. Three reverse gears."

The engine and the jeep's convulsions started again. For a moment we seemed stuck; then it inched a bit backwards, and with a rending of canvas, began to gather speed. I believe we came eventually through what had once been the roof, to find ourselves on top of it, with, all around us, the sidewalls still more or less standing. I saw something move under the canvas and for the second time that afternoon prayed that Sir George would not notice. This time I was heard. After all we had been through, the sagging sidewall seemed a minor obstacle. All three of us crouching down, we shot through it into the open air. The terrace was packed with people and at the sight of the jeep they began to struggle with each other at the main door. As we roared across the grass towards the drive Obe Jasus turned and waved. "We might as well say good-bye," he said.

IN the aftermath of our adventure at Monolough House Sir George's passion for music and for an audience seemed to increase. He invited a few more people out from town, and night after night we sat, terrorised and drunken, and, for the most part, musically ill-informed, at his feet. Appreciation of the music was shown in various ways. There were some who would pause, the glass raised halfway to their lips, with a slight frown between the eyes, until the conclusion of a particular passage. Some adopted masks of agony which suggested acute internal cramps. Some stared at the instrument itself, as if expecting the well-known smooth-haired fox terrier to emerge from the horn, head cocked. To comment was a chancy matter, whether one's level of musical knowledge was high or no. It was better to mime one's enjoyment. And besides the actuality I had my dreams, now nightly and unbroken, to contend with, which meant that I was exposed to music for fourteen hours or so out of the twenty-four. I decided that for sanity's sake I would have to leave.

I RETURNED to Dublin to find things greatly changed. Sir Mortlake had come into an unexpected legacy and returned to England, and The Warrens was no more. Eunice had departed to Paris, saying, apparently, that it could hardly be worse than Dublin. The closing of The Warrens was indeed a great blow. Gone was my broom-cupboard and my undulant mattress. Never again in that tiny space would I solace myself with the sages of the New World Bible. I faced now for the first time the problems of homelessness, but let me gloss over them; let me instead describe my next home, my next haven, which was to be mine until I was flung by chance or circumstance or the stars into the big world once more, as editor of a monthly magazine known as *The Trumpet*: though when I describe this home as mine I do so with the reservation that in its physical being it belonged to someone else, and that when I occupied it I was plagued a good deal by guests.

This new home soon came to be called "The Gurriers", from the number of people of that ilk whom it accommodated. Gurrier is a Dublin word I find it rather difficult to define. Not that it is not a word of precise application, in the sense that the justness or otherwise of that application is not immediately apparent, but that the gurrier elements in a personality can crop up in widely differing contexts. Thus, for instance, a Cabinet Minister can be, and frequently is, justly described as a gurrier; at least half the population of O'Turk's could be, and were, so described. An element of shiftiness is implied, and perhaps an element of braggadocio. A certain lack of respectability is almost certainly imputed, but with some unsuccessfully worn trappings of respectability: a double breasted suit, slightly wrong about the shoulders and slightly frayed at the rather wide trouser ends, would be more likely to be the uniform of a gurrier than the polo-neck and corduroys, though the latter certainly could be, and frequently were, also. On the other hand one could be completely disreputable and still not qualify for the appellation. An element of shabbiness of style, ready to degenerate at any moment into complete shamelessness of manoeuvre or approach, is certainly to be conveyed, but the word must on no account be confused with the word gutty, which simply means a low, loud-mouthed fellow from the slums. It would be hard to qualify for the appellation if one were genuinely and unmistakably remarkable: a person of extreme depravity or genius; on the other hand your ordinary, run-of-the-mill fellow in a pub would scarcely qualify either, unless by ordinary were meant ordinary, run-of-the-mill gurrier, for some, however slight, eccentricity or oddity of character, betraying an unusual if of course completely inaccurate view of the world, is implicit in the description also. Conscious knavery is not a necessary part of the meaning of the term, and a scrupulously honest gurrier is certainly conceivable; yet at the same time a scrupulously honest gurrier would certainly be a surprise. Most, if not all, of the O'Turk's beggars were gurriers.

"The Gurriers" was a shed of sorts, but it was a shed whose original function or *raison d'être* it would have been extremely hard to decide. It stood at the bottom of one of those long, overgrown gardens behind Baggot Street, which suggests, if I may hazard a joke, that it was a shed of the common, or garden variety, but it was by no means that. For one thing it was made of concrete, though with a corrugated iron roof, and it stood on its own, with four walls, being no sort of a lean-to. It had a door in the middle of one wall, and to one side of that door was a window which resembled an ordinary window except that no part of it was made to open. Thus, with its four concrete walls, its door and its window, "The Gurriers" was in a way more like a little house than a shed, and yet it was quite definitely not a little house either, for the interior was entirely bare and there was no fireplace, nor chimney, nor outlet for smoke; neither was there recess or cupboard or protuberance or angle, but simply the four concrete walls, the door, the fixed window, the corrugated iron roof and a concrete floor. There was nothing, that is to say, structural apart from these, for there was some furniture. The most outstanding article was a curious double decker iron bedstead, a perfectly plain, ordinary, old-fashioned bedstead, with tubular black structure and brass knobs, except that the structure was partly duplicated, like a freak of nature, and the brass knobs were consequently high in the air near the roof.

I acquired "The Gurriers" through the agency of a friend of mine who had recently, for want of anything better to do, set up in a small way as a contractor; hired some men from O'Turk's who had learned or purported to have learned carpentry and other minor arts in various gaols; and proceeded to outbid other, more orthodox and more established contractors for some sort of renovating job on the house to which the garden and shed were attached. He explained that he would gladly have let me sleep in the house while the renovating job proceeded, but that the activities of himself and his men would undoubtedly have been a disturbance to me, at least in the unseasonable hours of the morning, while I might possibly have been an impediment to them, to say nothing of the fact that the owner's representative might occasionally take it into his head to visit the house at night to see how the work was proceeding, and while I on my palliasse might conceivably have been explained away as a night-watchman, the explanation might not be found convincing. In the meantime he certainly hoped that the job—they were breaking the house up into plywood boxes, to be let at extravagant rents—would be protracted, and he was prepared to let me have the shed at the merely nominal rent of five shillings per week.

"The Gurriers" curious resemblance to a little house, albeit a little house without light, water, recesses or openable aperture for the egress of smoke or the ingress of oxygen, pleased me very much. I felt, for a short while at least, that I had a home, almost, as I say, a house, of my own. Access to "The Gurriers" in the daytime was through the big house, merrily resounding with hammerings, blasphemies and complaints. At night the big house was unfortunately locked up, I think to prevent the workmen sleeping or junketing on the premises, for fear, as I said, that the owner or his representative might drop in as they were passing. Then entrance and exit had to be effected over the garden wall, a feat not physically difficult for one could hoist oneself with the help of a wire guy that supported a telephone pole and various footholds in the wall, and descend by the roof of the shed and some boxes that I soon arranged. The only drawback about that was that it looked rather odd in daylight or the early hours of the evening, and quite suspicious if one should happen to be observed later in the night, nor was it easy to explain to the police the circumstances in which one lived. However, after a certain hour the lane was not very populous, being like most of the carriage lanes behind those broad Dublin streets, occupied mostly by little workshops and garages which closed reasonably early.

I am afraid, though, however houselike it was, that "The

Gurriers" had certain very definite disadvantages as a home; and that I tended to regard it as a poetic concept, something to be nested in the heart rather than very much frequented. I slept there at nights, certainly, but somehow, once one had emerged in search of one's morning cup of tea, there was an inclination not to go back until the possibilities of the day or the evening were absolutely exhausted. On a summer morning one could lie on, listening to the birds singing in the garden, looking at the roofs of the mews and the blue sky; but once out, you were out in the world, there was little doubt about it. It was nice to know one had a place, and a place that so much resembled an odd little house, but there was a tendency to try to get the day filled up without actually spending much time there. There was something just a little off-putting about the lack of the appurtenances of home, the gas-ring, the tap, the fire or anyway heater, which the miniature house-like charm of the place did not quite compensate for, at least circumstantially, though I thought of its existence often and gratefully during the day, and it much pleased me to think that I had as it were a secret, invisible house in the middle of the city.

Within a few weeks, however, my emotions were modified by an influx of beggary which destroyed at once my privacy and my poetic concept of the place. The laws of hospitality weigh much more heavily on the poor than on the rich. A man known to be penniless is not presumed to have earned the right to such temporary advantages or possessions as he may have. His standard of living is regarded as too low to be diminished; his comforts as too rudimentary to be disrupted by the presence of other people. He is in a weak moral position. Any mention of rights, or privacy, or possessions can be met with a sneer;

it is known that he has had little respect for these when the boot was on the other foot and he was wont to declare that necessity owned the loaf. His compassion is easily presumed upon because compassion is known to be part of his stock-in-trade. He who presumes upon the generosity of others can scarcely risk the allegation of ungenerosity himself. Besides, the very poor—and at this juncture I was certainly that—are easily tempted into communal living; the presence of other gentlemen of fortune is, in its way, a comfort; it may cost you ninepence today, but it may also provide you with sixpence tomorrow when your need for the sixpence is greater.

Anyway, I soon moved from the position of being a peripatetic guest into the equally invidious one of being a permanent host. Worse, instead of being an eccentric gentleman in reduced circumstances living in a mews or whatever—which, though few people had visited it, was known to be rather more picturesque than luxurious—I became simply one of a gang of down-and-outs living in a shed. Everything suffered. My self-esteem because I was now forced to witness my own emotions of irritation at the presence of unwanted guests: I who had so lately and blithely inveighed mentally against the hospitality of other hosts. I felt as a man who had been stripped of a cherished mental attitude, forced to recognise his own hypocrisy and to concede that the attitude has been bred out of self-interest. I was open to the charge—I levelled it at myself—of being a radical when it suited my needs, and a curmudgeonly reactionary now that I had acquired possessions. It was true that those other hosts were richer than I, that they had a great deal more space and that a guest was less of an infliction on them. I even tried to re-assure myself on the grounds that the guest had been I. But then

I had to admit that if they had more space, they had more to offer, and more to lose, that the proportions of advantage and disadvantage were roughly the same; that they had worked a great deal harder for their bigger structure than I for my little; that in short we were in the same case, and that I was turning out every bit as much of a begrudger as I had mentally reviled them for being: not, I can assure you, a very easy piece of knowledge to live with, and one that I am afraid reduced me to growling, jumping, nervous impotence, a surly unmanned host who could neither say stay with grace nor go with strength, whereas I had been better make the best of a bad job of it, one way or another.

Other things suffered besides my self-esteem and my essential picture of myself as one who didn't often have it but was decent when he did, that picture so dear to the heart of all beggars and so productive of spirit and openness in their dealings. My plans for "The Gurriers", plans so dependent on my poetic picture of it as a tiny secretive little house, went by the board. I had intended to cut or bore or cause to be bored a little more or less circular opening in the roof and to create, perhaps out of a slab of slate or something like that, a hearthstone, so that I could have a fire in the evenings. I had intended to canvass for at least, if not to purchase, a little oil-stove and the appropriate cooking utensils, and plates and the like of that. I had even imagined "The Gurriers" as festooned with two or three oil-lamps, a cosy, clean, warm and well-lit place where I could rejoice to sit in the evenings. But the presence of so many, the succession of so many, and such dilapidated, guests defeated these dreams. And remember, to be fair to myself now in my comparison of my attitude towards my guests with the attitudes of richer hosts I had known, that my guests were at the bottom of the scale. They were bright and cheerful enough occasionally in liquor or in funds, but they tended also to lie, all too apparent and all too present, in attitudes suggesting extreme lassitude and disinterest if not despair, under such coverings and in such corners as could be found, into the late hours of the morning and indeed the afternoon.

No, they did not help me to execute my plans for my little house with vigour and belief in their possible fruition; nor did their presence help such other plans as I may have had, such as that my sex-life, for example, could begin to flower in a different way and on a different soil now that I had a home for it, a lair where the basic privacies could be observed. My hopes in this direction had of course largely depended on my plans for the re-furbishing of the lair in question, for I could hardly expect the objects of my desire to lie delicately and deliciously under the coverings and on the bare mattress that at the beginning (and to the end too, alas) served me, but this is to say nothing of the fact that I could never be absolutely sure, once the rot had set in, of having "The Gurriers" free of guests for a single blessed evening, and the clumpings of the bed were not of course likely to be any the more satisfactory for the advent of clumpings on the roof.

I say once the rot had set in, for this state of affairs came about gradually. Once in the weakness or goodness—and which I can never be sure—of my heart I had admitted a guest I was ever more dithering and demoralised by demands made on me. "The Gurriers" remained unfurbished in the simple way I had set my heart on; the sight of a recumbent form or two—one in the lower berth of my bed as I stepped down in the morning and one perhaps on a palliasse in the corner—was not conducive to energy or discipline or ambition, and though the poor may comfort each other by companionship against the world, and even perhaps assist each other in moments of small crisis, they have, in some circumstances at least, also a demoralising effect on each other. And apart from such requests for hospitality as were frequently made on me at closing time in O'Turk's or the bona fides or at the close of a party, and apart from those who had got into the habit of assuming that they could count on "The Gurriers" as a last resort when, in the small cold hours of the morning all else appeared to have failed, a curious situation had arisen vis à vis my landlord—I mean my lessor—the contractor and his workmen. Being recruited from O'Turk's at minimal rates for such work as they were willing or able to perform, they were little better than beggars even now, indeed many of them came from the failures of the begging classes, demoralised back into work; and they were as yet, at least on the stipends offered, incapable of properly providing for themselves. Thus it came about that they were inclined to use "The Gurriers" as a sort of hostel, as if it had been a housing scheme adjacent to the job, laid on by a beneficent management with advanced ideas about industrial relationships, a Garden City suburb of the Cadbury kind. I am not sure how much my landlord may have connived at this development, having arrived at the idea perhaps in a sudden flash of inspiration, after he had let the place to me. I could see it was to his advantage, since it meant that they could live on less, in any case it meant that I was fighting on two fronts and that appeals for hospitality from this quarter could be backed up by its adjacency to the job and general handiness.

So, gradually, I abandoned my plans. I slept, almost fully clothed, as late into the morning as possible, and awoke under the hearthrug and the heavy window curtain (both found on the premises) which served me as covering, if not entirely without a sense of adventure, at least with one considerably dulled by the immediate difficulties to be faced. I could wash in the house where the work proceeded; I could perhaps lightly breakfast there off somebody's loaf of bread; if it was lunch-time there might even be tea. If the pub was thriving during the early sessions one was not too badly off; frequently one was invited for a snack during the holy hour; thereafter, if company fell off, I was quite content to spend a desultory afternoon in the National Library, perhaps having a bet or two round the corner if I had succeeded in laying my hands on any cash. Then it was the fortunes of war again for the session that ran roughly from five to eight, when the editor of *Further Horizons*, the Japanese, the Americans, the limeys, and the richer members of the company might depart to an evening meal, or even the accursed theatre. On the other hand they might not, and everything was fine until one woke again under the hearthrug.

By and large it was not so different from the life I had led as a grocer's intellectual, with the hearthrug standing in for the awakening to the job, and the blank hours and occasional hunger pains of the day representing the indignities of employment. It was not all roses by all means. There were boredoms, even small indignities, gaps to be faced on the nights when there wasn't a blessed sinner in the pubs, social calls proved fruitless or mentally impossible and one was faced with the abysmal prospect of a return to "The Gurriers", there to read, or perhaps even to write, by the light of the small oil-lamp which had been presented to me by a well-wisher and which reminded me all too clearly of the gradual atrophy of my hopeful plans. The New World Bible had somehow ceased to solace me since I had abandoned the life of action; and it seems to me now, looking back on it, that my mentality perhaps suffered from the lack of a corpus of thought to react against. I was in a way, I even suppose, in total sympathy with my environment.

IT seems to me now that things all round were not as good as they had been before my departure to Ardash. Perhaps the closing of The Warrens had something to do with it. I began to adventure more into other pubs, where I sometimes adopted a different persona and met a different class of person. I even occasionally visited the establishment where the regime intellectuals congregated. I caught a glimpse of the grocers' Secretary there once or twice, but I think my visits, apparalled as I then was, distressed him, for once when I came in he finished his drink and left the corner where he had been discoursing in Gaelic about that week's *New Statesman* immediately.

One morning, as I lay under my hearthrug in "The Gurriers", I heard approaching down the garden from the direction of the house a voice which was vaguely familiar.

"And is it here he is, in this little housheen? Well I wouldn't put it past him to have found a plaisheen like this where the song of the birds would inveigle the song out of him."

After a moment's cogitation I recognised this gibberish as belonging to a man called Ted O'Connell whom I had once or twice met in the Gaelic intellectuals' pub. He was, I knew, the boss of some state board or other: he administrated canals, or herrings, or limestone or something like that, and had the reputation of being wealthy and well-got in regime circles, but unfortunately, as I already knew, hard to touch.

As I wondered what had brought him to "The Gurriers" his long and Celtic face appeared at the window and I could see that he was accompanied by my landlord and a rather lesser type of intellectual civil-servant.

I bade them enter. Cigarettes were produced and the conversation began. O'Connell expressed astonished, delighted admiration for the circumstances in which I lived. It was, he said, a sight for sore eyes to see me here in my fastness, behind my walls. He referred to my poetic solitude, an ideal circumstance for the creation of "great spalpeens of poems", obviously unaware that I entertained guests day and night, and that two builders' labourers, a former rate-collector who was allegedly half-way through a gigantic novel about cattle-drovers, and another gentleman of uncertain profession who had been locked out by the whore with whom he was known to associate, had slept in my "fastness" the night before, and indeed but lately departed for the pubs. He even used the phrase "as snug as a bug in a rug" unblushingly, evidently unobservant of the fact that I was wrapped in one.

On our own removal to the pubs, however, it soon became apparent that behind the conversation lurked a moral imperative. They were all well-wishers, that was perfectly clear, and I shuddered in my broken shoes. The lesser civil-servant began by leading the conversation round to a friend of his, public relations officer for the gas-works or sewage system, I am not sure which. This was a sharp and talented man he declared, who wouldn't be a bit put out if he lost the job in the morning.

"Not a bit of him. Seumas could knock out a living as a free-lance journalist, starting tomorrow."

The possibilities of living by the pen were discussed. It was agreed that in Ireland things were very difficult. We had been joined by an auctioneer, whose brother was editor of the *Tipperaryman* and often contributed articles to the *Irish Independent*.

"He was always a lad for the writin', but except for he had the ould job it wouldn't keep him in butter."

This was to nobody's liking and the newcomer was soon reduced to a sulky silence. O'Connell held forth about the B.B.C. and the possibilities inherent in the Irish Radio were canvassed.

"Did you ever send anything to *The Trumpet*, Paddy?" he asked. "I'm sure you'd get a very sympathetic reception from Prunshios McGonaghy."

I shook my head dumbly.

"The brother often reads it," said the auctioneer. "I don't know though if he ever sends his stuff there. Leastways I don't ever remember him mintionin' it. Of course he has stuff here and there and you'd never hear a word out of him about it. I only discovered meself by accidint that he had an aarticil in the *Irish Digest* that was taken out of one of the provincial papers. He's not one to boast, not like a lot of others that go in for the writin'."

There was a stony silence. The rest of the company was afflicted by the greatest of conversational annoyances, a confusion as to levels.

O'Connell tried again. "I had a wordeen with Prunshios the other day, Paddy," he said. "He's looking for somebody like you to do a few aartic . . . , essays for him about a subject that's probably near to your own heart."

I assumed a mask of interest and enquiry.

"Mind you he's a bit out of touch, but his heart is in the right place. He'll listen to what you have to say."

"And what, might I ask," I asked, "would be the subject of these articles?"

"Well the fact of the matter is, Paddy, Prunshios is very interested in the younger generation, and he thinks, and I think, that you might be a spokesman for them. We old men, you know, with the best will in the world get a little bit out of touch and we don't know what you young fellows might be thinking. But we're anxious to learn. Oh, yes, we're anxious to learn all right. And you know, if you don't mind me saying so, I think it's your duty to tell us."

The company took an assenting sip, adam's apples registering grave agreement.

"Begod I don't know but they think at all," said the auctioneer. "Only interested in women and the like of that, as far as I can see." He congratulated himself by gesturing to the barman.

The day so far wasn't going too badly as days went, but I slipped in a sandwich on the auctioneer's round. There might well be agonies in store.

"I have a suspicion, Paddy, that there are a lot of things you'd be the better for getting off your chest. No use becoming too bitter, you know. I know you don't talk like my generation talked, nor Prunshios' either, for the matter of that, though our generations did a good job in their day. Oh they did a good job all right, and if you'll forgive me saying so, you young fellows should never forget it."

"Well, by God," said the auctioneer, "you said a true word there. If you ask me these young fellows take a hell of a lot for granted. It wasn't them that bate the tans."

"Oh well, be that as it may," riposted my friend, "I don't suppose they'd be found wanting either if the day ever came again. And for that matter Paddy here may well be serving the old sod better than you and I served it, though we did our bit. There's a time for everything in God's time, and, as Shakespeare himself says, God fulfils himself in many ways."

He smiled benignly on the company, his long Celtic face full of goodwill, and urbanely and cheerfuly ordered a drink in his turn, cracking a beneficent joke with the barman as he did so.

"You know," he said, suddenly serious again, "I often say this and as a matter of fact I was saying it to Prunshios himself only the day before yesterday when we were having a hand of cards together in the house of a mutual friend. There's more ways than one of serving your country, and Paddy here with his little poems and his intellect and his thoughts may well be striking a blow that future generations will think every bit as important as anything we ever did. I often feel we old fellows should have a bit more humility where the young are concerned. I'm not talking about understanding now, because to tell you the truth, Paddy, I don't pretend to understand a lot of the stuff that you young fellows are writing, but I think we ought to recognise our day is nearly done. Give the young their head. Let them think their own thoughts and say their own say. I'm not as young as I was, but bejabers I'm not one of those old fellows that thinks the younger generation does not respect Ireland and the Irish ideal, ay and love it too, as much as we ever respected or loved it, though again I'm proud to say we all did our bit, and it wasn't a bad bit either."

He smiled on the auctioneer. "Eh Ned? Don't you think it's time we old fellows took a back seat and gave the young men of Ireland their head?"

"Take the back of my arse," said the one enquired from. "Take the back of my arse and boil it. It wasn't the like of the youth of today that won the battle of Ballanagheer."

Silence washed in over this last remark, but my friend lost none of his urbanity and goodwill.

"You know," he said, "I've thought once or twice lately —and I know Prunshios agrees with me—that there may be a great wave coming, the like of the one that came thirty odd years ago." He laid his hand on my arm. "That it may be happening now, but that like the old men and the middle-aged men of those times, some of us may not be able to see what is happening, and that the youth may throw us aside as we threw the old fellows of those days. Don't get bitter, Paddy. Don't get bitter. Give us a chance. We're anxious to hear from you. We're anxious to help. We know you love your country. My God it makes my blood boil" . . . he did not deign to glance at the auctioneer . . . "it makes my blood boil to hear men of my own generation, who should know how we were misunderstood, ay and maligned, by men who I am the first to say had done their bit in their own day, abuse the youth of today without taking the trouble of understanding what they're up to, without trying to find out what is their vision of the national ideal." He smiled again. "Well now that's where I think you should give us a bit of help. We were young fellows ourselves once upon a time you know."

Apart from the anger that these insulting references to my alleged youth were causing me, I genuinely doubted that I could be any help. What, for example, was I up to? The plain fact of the matter was that I did not know. And what on earth was the national ideal? I accepted another drink and held my peace. My interlocutor continued.

"I was reading, you know, the other day a novel of

O'Faolain's," he said, the light of culture and civilisation in his eye. "Now O'Faolain is a man of my own generation almost. But you know his book is disillusioned. That's the only word for it, disillusioned. Now oddly enough I think that marks him out as a member of my generation, not of yours. For you know I believe that if there is one thing the youth of today are not, it's disillusioned. If there's one thing the youth of today are, it's"—for an instant I thought he was about to say illusioned, or perhaps deluded, but he avoided the trap. "If there's one thing the youth of today are, it's too full of ideals. They may be unharnessed ideals. They may even be wrong ideals, though that's as may be, and it's maybe not for us old fellows to say. But I'll tell you something Paddy, when I saw the place you were living in this morning, the place you have chosen to write in, and to think in, and where may be the next revolution in Irish thought will come from, it made me feel very humble. Very humble indeed."

"Well begod I don't know anything about that," said the auctioneer, "not having seen the apartment. But as far as humility goes, our friend here seems to have his share of it, for he's too humble to buy a drink anyway."

The monopoly administrator seriously supplied the deficiency, while the auctioneer survived a paroxysm of self-congratulatory, bronchial laughter.

"I want you to promise me one thing, Paddy," my friend continued. "That you will ring up Prunshios McGonaghy. That you will think about what he has to say. And that when he asks you, as he will ask you, to write this article for him, that you will speak your piece like a man."

Dumbly, glass in hand, I promised.

"I'm not sure Paddy, that we haven't made mistakes. Not at all sure. I'd be the first to admit that here is a very definite sense in which we might be said to have failed. Indeed yes. I remember, thirty-five years ago, Mellows saying to me: 'Ted, have you ever envisaged the possibility of failure?' And you know it didn't strike me till long afterwards what he meant. When we were on hunger strike in nineteen hundred and thirty-three I was discussing with some of the boys what had happened to the national ideal, when it suddenly struck me that what Liam meant was that we might fail after we had won. And you know, to a man of my generation, that was a terrible thought."

Comforting himself with another large whiskey, and magniloquently including the company in his gesture, my regime friend continued his, to me somewhat obscure, discourse.

"That's the thought that haunts me, Paddy, and troubles more than one man of my generation. And that's what only you can tell us. For our success or failure in terms of the national ideal depends to a great extent on how the young feel about Ireland. Oh I know all about the emigration figures and that sort of thing. That doesn't matter. That's only a matter of economic re-organisation, and sooner or later we'll find the answer to that. What I want to know is, do you feel that your generation has come closer to the national ideal than ours, or not?"

He beamed on me gently but interrogatively.

"Begob I don't believe he'd even get close to an each-way treble from the looks of him, or a you-know-what on a starry night, unless he got his hair cut. I have a young fellow meself at the university goin' on to be a B.Comm. and 'jabers I don't know where he got half the notions he's picked up. 'Twasn't in the good Catholic household where he was reared anyway. The youth of today would be a sore disappointment to Rory and Liam and Cathal Bruagha

I'm thinkin'. God that young fellow of mine gives me the colic every time I look at him."

Silently, seriously, albeit smilingly enduring, my administrator of inland waterways or otherwise continued to gaze at me interrogatively. I fell back on the only line of defence available.

"I think I'd rather answer that in writing," I said.

"And spoken like a writer too," he twinkled. "I wouldn't doubt you. Oh, we'll get something worth reading when you and Prunshios get together. Now, remember I'll tell him you'll be ringing him up. And strictly entre nous as the saying goes, I don't think you'll find him ungenerous. And you won't mind me saying, Paddy, that there never was a poet yet—and I've known a few in my time, oh yes, I knew Fred Higgins and Colum and the lot—that wasn't the better for a few pounds in his pocket. Not that it stays there very long. Oh, I know the poets. Give us four more large ones there, Mick, like a good fellow."

THUS, *nolens volens*, was I thrust into the world once more. Not immediately of course, nor very dramatically to begin with. But the germ, the thought of fairly loose cash allegedly waiting, once sown would not uproot itself. I made such enquiries as I could about Prunshios McGonaghy. I asked Mahaffey, a poet friend of my acquaintance. "Meanest man ever shat," he declared. "An ould bollocks who wouldn't give you the steam off his piss. You'd be better off writin' bettin' dockets than writin' for that ould fraud." McGonaghy was known to have left-wing leanings and was vaguely associated in my mind with arson, murder, treason and battles long ago. I asked a revolutionary whom I knew, one of a slightly older vintage than was general in O'Turk's. "Doctrinaire," he said. "Not flexible enough to understand contemporary conditions. Not in touch with revisionist thought." That wasn't much help, but in my fumbling, half-hearted way I attempted to ring the great man at his office. I had a vague idea that I might so manoeuvre a conversation or a meeting as to get some cash without writing any gibberish whatever. And of course I knew all too clearly that if I did attempt to write anything, gibberish it would be.

The phone calls resulted in a great deal of nervous anxiety for the reason that there never seemed to be anybody at the other end. Thus the nerving up process had to be gone through twice a day for at least a week, while the factitious guilt grew steadily. Before the week was over I had of course lost all real ambition about the money or anything else. All that drove me on was the pseudo-moral compulsion which I shall have occasion to refer to again when I come to deal with my relationship with the B.B.C., a pseudo-moral compulsion about which I will only say here that it is founded on a putative remorse, centred somewhere in the future, for not following the line of putative advantage which in the world's eyes had opened out before one, a remorse centred in the future when the opportunity had gone, but felt at the time as keenly as if one were already tasting the bitter fruits of one's neglect, and this although one's every instinct was crying out against the step which this obscure amalgam of imagined public opinion and one's own worse judgment was dictating. How was one to prove, to others perhaps, but more important to oneself, so often neglectful, that one's inactivity was not a matter of mere neglect?

Finally, however, the phone was answered. I knew the person in question could not be Prunshios McGonaghy, because I knew that Prunshios McGonaghy hailed from the North, whereas this man had an unmistakable Dublin accent. Beyond this assumption, however, I could not find any firm ground at all, for whoever he was, he was exclusively pre-occupied with some grievance of his own, to do with somebody referred to as "that old cunt". Was this a reference to McGonaghy? I could not find out, since my unknown prolocutor, once embarked on his theme, whatever it was, brushed my queries briskly aside, but my premonitions were not put to sleep when he ended his discourse by declaring: "I hear the old bollocks on the stairs now. I know his step. Oh I know his step if any man does. And you mark my words, if you have anything to do with that old cunt, you'll regret it. He's left a trail of dead men behind him wherever he went." Whereupon he abruptly rang off.

This, if it did refer to McGonaghy, was hardly reassuring, but I was still obscurely driven on. At length I actually took to visiting the offices, or so-called offices, of *The Trumpet*, and there one day I was lucky, for just as I arrived on the landing a man shot out of the door, his neck extended in front and his coat-tails flying behind. He came to a halt in the corridor and peered at me suspiciously. He was more or less the right age, but there was something in his dress and appearance, his bald head perhaps, his steel-rimmed spectacles, or his old-fashioned winged collar, which betokened that he lived by other myths than did Prunshios McGonaghy.

"Are you lookin' for the old bollocks?" he enquired, his

eyes blue and piercing over the glasses. As non-committally as possible, I affirmed that I probably was.

"You'll not find him here," he said. "You'll not find him here. That fellow has bigger fish to fry. This is only tuppence ha'penny stuff to that fellow. I don't know what he's up to. I don't know what he's up to at the moment, mind you, but he's up to something. He's been back and forward to London twice in the last month. He hasn't hardly taken his arse out of the airplane before he's off again. Off again, mark you. That fellow's very, very deep, and it's very, very hard to know sometimes what the hell he's up to, but mark you this. Mark you this." He prodded me with a long bony finger. "Whatever the bloody hell he's up to, he's up to no good, and there's somebody will suffer for it before he's finished. Oh yes, somebody will suffer, and it won't be him. I'll tell you something, and I'm not telling you a word of a lie now. That fellow has left a trail of dead men behind him wherever he went." As he made this last allegation, his eyes achieved a quite startling shade of blue. Then, to my mind somewhat inconsistently, he added:

"Come on to hell out of here before the old fucker comes in. I thought a couple of minutes ago I heard his step on the stairs." He looked at me suspiciously as if it was possible that I was up to something too. "It must have been yourself I heard." He put both his palms together, then shot one forward as if leaving the other standing. "It's easier to get away from him if you meet him on the stairs. I'm in dread and terror these days he'll trap me in the office. Sometimes my nerves gets so bad, not knowing what the hell he's up to, that I can't talk to him at all. And he has me in such a state at the moment that I keep hearin' his step on the stairs every minute of the day."

He was urging me towards the stairhead as he spoke.

"But," I said, "I do want to see the old . . . the man."

"You don't want to see him. You don't want to see him. I'll tell you all there is to be known about that fellow, barrin' what he's up to at the moment, for that I don't know I'll tell you frankly, except that he's up to no good, and he has me nearly demented with the guessing. You don't want to see him, not if you value your life. I'll tell you all you need to know about him—only for the love of God let us get out of here quick for I keep hearing his step on the stairs."

I allowed myself to be shepherded downwards. In the street my new-found friend asked if I would mind paying a visit to the betting-shop around the corner to see the results of the two-thirties.

He stared morosely at the boards for a moment or two, then turned and gazed at me worriedly over the glasses.

"I swear to God that fellow Fallaps is up to some very deep game," he said, "for he hasn't had a winner for four weeks. And whatever hookey business he's up to, that 'Tightrein' fellow is in cahoots with him, for he tips every bloody runner he has."

We went to the pub. It turned out that my suspicious friend worked for *The Trumpet*, or perhaps, to put it more exactly, for Prunshios McGonaghy. It appeared he was circulation manager, advertising manager, correspondence clerk, accountant, and, to a startling extent, at the moment, editor. He had been associated with Prunshios—"I know the old bollocks if any man does, but sometimes he has me so demented with wondering what he's up to that I'm not telling you a word of a lie I can't sleep at nights"—in a variety of enterprises, literary, commercial and political, since they had been in gaol together during the troubles.

There appeared to have been times in the long years when he had descended to the role of plain pensioner. At others, as for instance at the moment, he had been required to undertake a multiplicity of jobs of an uneasily defined nature.

"Whatever that old cunt is up to, it's nothing to do with *The Trumpet*, I can tell you. He doesn't give a lick of his, if you'll forgive me, arse for *The Trumpet*. That's only a front. He's fishin' in deeper waters. And do you know sometimes when I'm lyin' awake at night, I wonder will he over-reach himself. He bears a charmed life, that I do know, but he's bound to over-reach himself sooner or later."

And apart from information, or alleged information, about his employer, my friend, whose name was Casey, gave me also some advice. "You write whatever the hell comes into your head, but mention Ted O'Connell in the note, for he's deep in Ted O'Connell's pocket."

I explained the difficulty of writing anything at all on the required subject.

"Don't bother your barney about that. That's neither here nor there. Oftentimes when I'm worried or depressed or he has me bothered not knowin' where he's delvin', I think of the old days when we were children and went to the seaside, and I think of the sea, and I sort of let my thoughts flow, just flow on like. That's the way to do it. Just choose something that freshens the mind and let yourself ramble on like. That chancer is no more interested in what goes into *The Trumpet* at the moment than he is in blessin' himself. Mind you, mind you, tomorrow or the next day, when his schemes have collapsed, or maybe he's brought them off, he'll come roarin' into that office like a mad bull and torment me from mornin' till night, but for the moment, for the moment mark you, he's deep in hookey business of some dark shade or description. Don't tell me. Don't tell me. I know him."

THIS advice, though excellent as I could see, proved difficult to follow. It was hard to find time for an extended prose-discourse of the kind indicated. It was the usual problem of the writer: live horse and you'll get grass. In the meantime I had to subsist, and the only way that could be done was to spend the major part of the day in the pub. Again I felt that false guilt, that social guilt, that shame about lacking the expected responses to the knock of opportunity, that worry about one's inability to justify one's neglect to an imaginary, sensible well-wisher. At last, however, in weariness and agony of mind, in an orgy of utter self-disgust, I concocted some rubbish and sent it off to Prunshios McGonaghy with a note referring (for my disgust at this point was even more acute) in somewhat occluded terms to my conversation with O'Connell.

To my surprise the response was instantaneous. The author of the missive I received had been waiting to hear from me. There was a definite air of reprimand. I had been remiss about ringing him up. I was bidden to the premises of *The Trumpet* on the morrow; and there in some confusion of spirit I went.

There was nobody in the tiny office when I arrived, though the door was not locked, so I sat myself down and read some letters. I had some vision of what Prunshios McGonaghy would be like, not only from Casey's description but from the tweedy, Marxist novels about peasants and fishermen I had read many years before; and when eventually the notorious footsteps were heard on the stairs and the door was thrust open, he was more or less as I had imagined him: a huge, grey, lean and fevered man, dressed all in black like an Irish politician of the old school. He came into the tiny office like a man about to address a meeting in a draughty hall, a meeting of insubordinate supporters, a man who was late, earnest and angry, his hands thrust into the pockets of his long, black frieze coat; took off the wide-brimed black hat which is the standard uniform of the patriotic man of letters in Ireland, and flung himself into the chair, abandoning his air of stern haste for one of tired greatness, weariness and contempt.

"Good morning," I said.

"Good morning be dommed. What the hell is the motter with all you yong men?"

I found no reply. There was so much the matter with me and so much of it unbelievable: troubles of the heart and of conscience, ills of the flesh, the poverty of the grave.

He pulled open two or three drawers, swept some papers impatiently to the floor, retrieved what I recognised immediately from its awful condition as my manuscript and flung it on the desk. "I don't feel the fresh wund of your mind blowing through this," he said.

"The fresh what?" I ventured in unaffected anxiety.

"The fresh wund. The fresh, free gale of your mind is not blowing in this. It's not forward looking." He glared at me. "Are you wurred in?" he demanded.

"Wurred what?" I said, though I meant it the other way round.

"Wurred in—wurred in to life. None of you yong fellas are wurred in to life. Where do you live?"

I told him. In a shed at the bottom of somebody's garden,

in company with a floating population who begged in the same pub and who, whatever else they were, were certainly not wurred in.

He snorted, "Tick, tick," he said. "How do you expect to know anything about the movements of the dialoctic in a place like that? It's appalling, nothing short of appalling. If it were the slums now . . ." He snapped his jaws shut. "Get out of there immediately," he said, "and get a room in a slum."

"But," I said innocently, "it is a slum."

"It's the wrong kind of slum," he roared. "Ye'll not have yer finger on the pulse of the people in a place like that."

I tried to explain that I actually spent very little time in the place, what with begging in the pub, reading in the National Library and other activities.

"Matter a domm," he shouted. "It's as plain as the nose on yer face that yer not . . ." He sought for a metaphor. I was to realise in time that his stock was limited. His eye fell on the telephone. He picked it up, base and all, and held it aloft. "Yer not wurred in," he declared triumphantly. At that instant, held up at arm's length as it was, the instrument began to ring. He slammed it down on the desk and scowled at it ferociously; then, making no effort to answer it, he picked up his patriotic hat and strode impatiently to the door, gesturing me to follow.

"We'll talk in the coffay," he declared, glaring at the telephone, "about being wurred in."

In the coffay, a monstrous, gilded place over a cinema, he was a changed man, flirting with elderly waitresses, saluting parish priests jovially, ordering a revolting plate of cakes for me as if I were a favourite nephew out on a treat, laughing with his teeth at his own jokes.

Suddenly he became serious. "Ye must objectivise the situation," he said. "Ye must learn to see it as part of the historical process. I want to feel the cutting edge of your mind on your problems."

The cutting edge of my mind had in fact long since given up my problems in despair, and nowadays it confined itself to making faint gnashing noises in the middle of the night, but I forebore.

"I want to feel from your writing that you feel you're part of the dialoctic process. I'm going to rescue you. I'm going to make you a part of the main stream of Irish life, so that your mind will become as infollible a guide to the forward-looking elements in the prosent, historical, dialoctic situation as . . . as MacMurkagaun's," he concluded, naming a minor peasant novelist of the day. He paused, flung out an arm and seized a passing parish priest. Was mother Church to be enlisted to aid this project? I wondered, but it was only an exchange of pleasantries of the cloth, lay and clerical, dialoctic and theological, and of tips for the dogs at Harold's Cross. "Ond we're winning the battle for world peace," he shouted, pumping the reverend gentleman's hand in farewell, swung back to me and demanded: "Are ye wulling to consider it if I can arrange it with——? " He named a politico known to have cultural aspirations.

I did not know quite what I was supposed to consider and visions of varying probability came to me. He had, I now knew, a lot of friends in high places, old republican comrades through whom he shared in the proceeds of certain of the smaller state monopolies: clay-pipes, horn rosary-beads, shamrock for Americans. Casey had given me the general picture. Was I to be made director of one of these enterprises? Or was I, more likely, to be offered a hazardous and minor task, to be asked for example to smuggle shamrock into England during an epidemic of foot and mouth disease, making endless return trips on the Liverpool boat, amid the smell of puke, and porter, and the strains of Galway Bay? Surely not, I thought, on reflection; we are, after all, men of letters, and the main stream must be a literary matter. He is going to give me a contract for articles on emigration, inshore fishery, re-afforestation, rural depopulation, housing conditions. I could see my days passing in a miasma of misinformation, a damp fog of inaccurate and out-of-date statistics. But Prunshios banged the table so that the cutlery jumped, the waitresses glared and about forty parish priests turned warning glances in our direction.

"The key to the whole matter," he shouted, "is in the rubbish-boskets."

"The rubbish-boskets?" I queried with that look of intelligent anticipation which is the stock-in-trade of aspiring subordinates. He became confidential.

"Do you realise thot there are twonty thousand rubbish-boskets affixed to lomposts in the coty of Dublin?"

"Twonty thousand!" I breathed in admiration, but still in the dark.

"Twonty thousand," he repeated emphatically. "And overy one of them can be a wondow for the forward-looking mind. Twonty thousand at ten and sixpence is eighteen thousand . . ." His lips moved in a silent rapture of calculation, while I gazed at him across the cups, his empty for the third or fourth time, mine still full to the brim, with the bedraggled remains of a cigarette afloat in the cream.

He outlined his plan. It appeared that there really were twenty thousand rubbish boskets affixed to lamposts in the city of Dublin; that his friend the politico, then serving a routine term of office as Alderman, had, as a gesture to

Irish literature, offered him an exclusive right to the letting of advertising space on these boskets, the proceeds to be devoted to the expansion and resuscitation of *The Trumpet*; that I was to be the principal agent of this renaissance; that, in short, I was being offered the post of Associate Editor.

The fatal step is taken because we are hypnotised and weak; rarely, if ever, because we are really the victims of circumstance. Prunshios was waving a roll of tenners the size of a bookmaker's ransom in the air, my eyes, the eyes of the parish priests and the eyes of the waitresses following every oscillation. He peeled off a tenner. "Here's a month's salary in advance," he said. "Ye'll need to buy a few things and get a room for yourself. Here, lassie, give us the bill and congrotulate this yong fella on the future." He hurled back his chair.

"Don't stir, don't stir. Finish yer cakes. Finish yer cakes."

He advanced towards the cash desk in a whirl of activity, frieze coat, fistful of tenners, patriotic hat and slaps on the back for chosen parish priests all flying about.

At the swing-doors he turned. "Get a room in a slum," he shouted. "A real slum. Get wurred in."

He was gone and I was an editor, a wage-slave once more: the richer by a tenner it is true, but an editor nonetheless. I sat alone among the somnolent clergy, brooding on the awful fact, while the heel of my cigarette luxuriated in the cream.

AND being an editor with Prunshios, though of course theoretically a great improvement on my former state, was not on the whole pleasant. I was not the right man for the job, though looking back on it now I find it a little difficult to name the quality, if that is the word, which I lacked. Optimism, perhaps?

The Trumpet had been a smart literary and sociological magazine during the war, when it had been edited by a peasant historian rather more sophisticated than Prunshios, and when Ireland itself had been the home of flourishing artistic movements. It had carried a deal of documentary reportage and statistics about fishing, as well as poems like abbatoirs, full of bones and sinews and thighs and hearts, and jerky short-stories about unevenly articulate peasants whose utterances varied from monosyllabic grunts to phrases like, " when you shook out the bright scarf of your laughter ".

It had not thrived under Prunshios. For one thing, with the end of the war the cattle-boats had been crammed with departing writers, standing knee-deep amid the puke and porter, quietly forgetting about O'Flaherty and O'Faolain and rehearsing their line on Connolly, Kierkegaard, Kafka and Scotty Wilson. For another, he lacked, let's face it, the flair. He had perhaps too many things on his mind, what with the dialoctic, dog-racing on alternate nights at Harold's Cross and Shelborne Park, shadowy creditors preventing his attendance at the office, and former republican comrades outstripping him in the minor monopolies racket, while he clung, with a strange and chivalrous obstinacy, to his outmoded and ever more confused marxist opinions. Casey alleged darkly that his only interest in the continued existence of *The Trumpet* was so that hollowed-out bundles of it could be used to smuggle some mysterious small articles into England, but even for this some sort of circulation was necessary, and it was when the circulation was falling to practically nothing barring the mythical hundreds for whom the hollow copies were destined that I was called in, having been recommended by O'Connell as an up and coming young man. But besides the danger to the smuggling trade Prunshios was quite genuinely, like many who have long since abandoned composition themselves, motivated by a desire for a movement. And also there was the Alderman, a person of similarly confused opinions, presumably expecting great things to come of his rubbish-boskets.

Prunshios would summon me to a coffay and make the most impossible demands about the availability of the so-called young.

"Have ye found the seeds yet?" he would shout, as if I had mislaid them somewhere. Then he would mix the metaphor. "If you let the fresh wund of your mind blow through *The Trumpet* ye'll find the seeds springing up everywhere. You can bring great things to birth," he would declare, but his eye had begun to wander uneasily. Fortunately, whether his schemes were progressing favourably or otherwise, and whether indeed the long-awaited overreaching was coming to pass, he was seldom in the office and most of our meetings took place in the accursed coffays, where, always, surrounded by droves of parish priests, Prunshios would sit, solemnly, indeed threateningly discussing whether I was more or less wired in than last time. Though the light of desperation was growing in his eye, this seemed to increase his generosity rather than diminish it, and though my wage would have put most of the more salubrious slums out of reach, a whole tenner was sometimes the reward for an editorial conference in a coffay.

We differed of course on fundamental issues, if indeed I can describe my silent fumblings and Prunshios's long-decided-on oratorical devices as capable of any such thing as a difference. But beyond that my troubles were circumstantial. Editor though I was, I was still living in "The Gurriers", still surrounded by the recumbent forms of underpaid stir-carpenters and general layabouts, an abyss of cheerful beggary which somehow seemed to make Prunshios' social pre-occupations less forceful to my mind than they might otherwise have been. I had also been knocked rudely out of the position of worthy recipient of drink into that of unworthy purveyor, so that I was generally worse fed and in worse health than I had been before our fateful original interview. It was hard indeed to muster up enthusiasm for the extension of the carrigeen moss industry, or the possible utilisation of the various parts of the herring's anatomy, down to the tail and the fin, in portable, prefabricated factories, themselves made of herring-bone cement, along the west-coast, when one was circumstantially situated as I was.

ANOTHER result of my new status, and one which sapped my energies to an appalling extent, was that I was now presumed in some quarters to be a rational human being, capable of choice, action and the disposition of forces. Decisions were urged on me in spheres far from the offices of *The Trumpet*. Structure breeds structure. A man who acquires a motor-car is in some danger of acquiring a garage; and it is after all a small step from that to having a house.

Since my return from Ardash I had begun to conduct one or two affairs of the heart in what I flattered myself would be a sufficiently distant and innocuous fashion to give everybody the minimum of trouble. I meant to take, and to continue, whatever transpired, taking, full advantage of my status as beggar, that is as a man whose freedom of action and movement is known to be limited, who can lay no far reaching plans and come to no epoch-making decisions. And where before, when my status of beggar was known and accepted, I had hoped to be allowed to conduct these affairs in a way that suited my then disposition and reserves of strength down to the ground, that is to say to allow them to conduct themselves in the remotest and most tenuous fashion, scarcely visible to the naked eye, hardly noted in the dossiers, barely to be accounted for in the introspective hours before the dawn, I was now plunged into what for me—though perhaps it would not have been for others—was a veritable whirl of intrigue, a malaise of initiative and suggestion, far, far removed from the nebulous liaisons, the calm anticipations, the explainable paralysis, the manifest impossibilities of reaching any final conclusion which I had hoped would be the happy lot of beggary. In short, my protestations were now presumed to have the backing of cash and status.

Let me say at once that in this matter I believe enthusiasm to be the chief enemy. I have been berated, as the reader knows, in other contexts for my lack of enthusiasm: my grocing, my music-loving, my editing, all were performed, I admit it, in a droiling, lagging fashion, not at all what was required. On the other hand my protestations of love were foolishly enthusiastic. I can only attribute the growth of this unfortunate failing to the circumstances of beggary and its freedoms. A beggar cannot conceivably be taken up on the matter whatever gibberish he mouths. In the old days of Eunice I had caused myself some trouble by this weakness, this debility of sense. It was nothing to what began to loom before me now. And though the title, "Assistant to the Secretary" had raised perhaps some honest hopes in Bridget, their worldly aspect cannot have been too overpowering, for, after all, for all the dear girl knew, there might have been twenty assistants to the secretary, each one paid less than the other, down to the twentieth, who was me: certainly my appearance and general financial state would suggest an ill-rewarded post whose prospects were of the darkest. Unfortunately, when I took rank as an editor, I still had the habits of beggary without its freedoms. At one bound, I had been lifted high among the intellectuals of the regime. Peculiarities of clothing, absence of cash, chronic weaknesses of one kind or another, could all be put down by an understanding woman to one's intellectual avocations. A firm but gentle hand on the reins and whatever needed remedying could be remedied.

The reader must remember the peculiarities of the place and the time. In the case of Bridget and Eunice I had enjoyed what were almost, apart from marriage or adultery, the only two forms of relationship available in that time and in that place. Whichever one had exhibited me as more wurred in to living I cannot say, but they were opposite and extreme ends of a dilemma. On the one hand were the native girls, fresh, desirable, but almost adamant in their chastity; on the other those females who were available without mind-darkening commitments, generally immigrants, and almost certainly with the dew well and thoroughly brushed off them. The difficulty was in enjoying, at one and the same time, an orthodox romantic illusion and an orthodox sensual satisfaction. You will say to me that this is a perennal difficulty, and such is human nature that it undoubtedly is; yet I speak now, not of an obstacle to romantic love that is inherent in the cross-grained human heart, but of a local and circumstantial annoyance, a matter of sociology, history and religion, which had to be overcome before one could luxuriate in the general sadness of the human condition. Protected by their religious beliefs, their virginal underclothing, their atavistic yearning for certain reassurances, the young, the glowing, the nice girls would yield as an almost general rule but certain partial and limited satisfactions, and those only after a great deal of fuss and bother for which I no longer had the energy, or, for that matter, the acquaintance.

Of course if one was prepared to countenance adultery one could perhaps foster the romantic emotion and obtain a fitting reward, indeed the obstacles would ensure that the emotion throve in spite, even, of the universal difficulty I have mentioned. Here perhaps lay the combination desired, of youth and readiness, of circumstance accounted and provided for, of beauty and freshness sufficient to provoke the desired emotion and a sensual fulfilment to boot. So I had begun, in a faltering but enthusiastic fashion, to trespass on other people's preserves. Yet this solution, at first sight so plausible, proved now to have unlooked-for terrors. Apart from my accursed weakness for romantic protestation, the relationship in itself has an inherent, swiftly gathering, and eventually terrifying momentum of protestation of its own. The combination of the two was extreme and ridiculous. There was neither rhyme nor reason to it. And this only at the beginning, when it would have needed special instruments to record any action on my part. It was not, as I say, so bad so long as I was protected by patent poverty; the moment I acquired status I was plunged, suddenly and most unexpectedly, into crisis.

None of the girls concerned had any clear idea, I am convinced, of the gap between my status and my true circumstances. Assured, nay, wildly misled, by the protestations hurled about, they believed it lay within my power to make my way at all hours of the day and night to obscure and remote places of assignation; they little understood that, so far from being able to carry them off, frequently mere minimal mobility lay beyond me, that I might not be able to avail myself even of public transport and that my shoes might be in such a condition as to render walking in the rain exceedingly dangerous, particularly when the now chronically undermined state of my health is taken into account as well.

Fouled up as I was, and with dangers yawning at my feet, I began to seek once more for yet another alternative to the Eunice-Bridget duality, and it was some months and much soul-searching after the fateful morning when I had been routed out of bed by the administrator of electricity or whatever he was, that I met Anne. She was a widow, her husband having been one of six victims in a multiple car-crash on the way back from the bona fides one Saturday night. Childless and still very young, she lived with an unmarried brother in the Booterstown area, and was the centre of an admiring circle of his bourgeois friends, on whom the suggestion of fragility and secret daring, of pliancy and licentiousness, which her particular kind of blondeness and anatomical structure often conveys to the male, seemed to have a particularly deleterious effect. Unfortunately, as so often happens in courtship, I was compelled to a large extent to enter their circle; indeed in my case the compulsion was greater than usual, for my difficulties in entertaining off my own bat were, as I hope I have made clear, extreme.

The brother was a decent fellow, and liberal with drink; and for Anne I rapidly conceived a certain fondness; the friends I must say here and now were an intolerable crew. They frequently foregathered in certain fashionable hostelries in the centre of the city, lounge bars where every surface stared back at the eye, or tiled and marbled graveyards attached to hotels and restaurants, and they were great eaters of steak, onions and potatoes. Being desirous to see the girl I would make a tour of their haunts, and come across them eventually perhaps, after parting with some hard-earned shillings in the search, grouped round one of the shiny tables, the men hunched animatedly on the small stools, their split jackets hanging over the edge, one split or two splits, according to whether they were solicitors, surveyors, veterinary surgeons, doctors, engineers or auctioneers. The conversation would then proceed something as follows.

"Hello, Mick." (That was the brother.)

"Ah, the hard. What'll you have?"

"Bottle of stout. Hello Anne."

"Hello, Paddy."

"Hello." (This to the rest of the company, the response being a series of glum nods.)

The brother: "Push over there and let the man sit down."

Anne: "Sit here, Paddy."

Momentary silence all round, and then gradually they would get back into gear. The metaphor is apt, for their conversation consisted mostly of bore and stroke, crank and cam, cubic capacity and developed horse-power. "Oh, they're a good lively job, there's no doubt about that, they're very fast up through the gears, they've got a nice dicey touch to them, but I'd rather have the old M.G. any day of the week. It's all motor-car." A certain facility in the deployment of technical terms allowed me occasionally to partake in this kind of chat, and indeed, since I knew it was the hire-purchase companies, Bowmakers perhaps, or the British Wagon Company, who really owned all the motor-cars concerned, I saw no reason why not; but sooner or later I would go too far and be exposed in the middle of a heated argument as an impostor and a chancer. This made me unpopular, but little I cared; I was unpopular enough already.

During the early days of my courtship, if I may so refer to it, it was, I am convinced, the settled opinion of the whole company that I came among them looking for free drink. Their rounds were far beyond me, being perhaps paid for by the British Wagon Company also, so I rarely or never bought one, and it was a great point of honour with them to put one up like men. This made things difficult, though I really had no alternative in the beginning but to work under cover of the general *bonhomie* and pursue the acquaintance in the best way I could. The brother was literary in a mild way, being interested in the drama, a form of artistic endeavour with which I believe he confused my own humble activities, and he encouraged me. As for the others, you can get used to anything they say; they got used to me in time; and I soon grew to be on first-name terms with the lot. They were tolerant enough on the surface, and though my unpopularity never diminished, and was to grow very rapidly in the weeks ahead when it became obvious that I had reached some sort of an understanding with Anne, they put up with me for a while. I would be swept, unpopular but tolerated, to the bona fides, and afterwards included with the sugar bags in a car bound for the residence in Booterstown, where they would continue their heated discussions of motor-cars far into the night. There I would press my suit, ignoring the glowerings and the mutterings as far as was humanly possible. Anne received my compliments and returned my hole-and-corner caresses with evident pleasure, but I was confronted with the next move and that was not easy to make. There were for one thing too many people about; I had intruded on their territory; the ferocity of their reaction was difficult to gauge.

We began to meet privately in obscure boozers up by the canal, in the nearer and more ancient suburbs, even on the North Side, sitting enislanded in the middle of huge and horrible lounge bars made of plywood upholstered in red leatherette. As a rule Anne paid for the drinks, and this brought us closer together; but she still had no clear idea of my circumstances and put, I think, everything that puzzled her down to the notorious instability of my kind. Then I secured private ingress into the house at a time when, according to her almost unspoken but definite assurance, the brother would be absent, and so at last I enjoyed her.

The first occasion was in early summer, and I came by arrangement about six o'clock. I had tried to make it the afternoon and I do believe that shocked her. I have an acute horror of the suburbs, but this time even the raw white concrete roadways, the thin new houses with their black drainpipes, the god-forsaken bus-stops and the gangs of little boys in the caps and blazers of their noxious schools failed to strike terror into me. We both, I think, knew what I had come for, but as she offered me whiskey and went through the motions of making tea for herself she masked her knowledge behind an elaborately trivial flow of chatter that was only slightly, if unmistakably, more nervous and gay than that which might have eased an ordinary social call. As she perhaps partly and perversely hoped, it almost delayed me too long, but we had been through the preliminaries often enough with the brother's parties for background, and the stages now were easy. I divested her, in jest and earnest, of the light woollen jumper and the skirt she wore. She declared, quite understandably, that she felt—though she did not look—ridiculous pretending to drink tea half naked in the kitchen, and took me, her clothes in one hand, my palm in the other, to her bedroom, her buttocks oscillating delightfully under her panties as she climbed the stairs two steps ahead of me. The suggestion of an extreme feminine willingness to comply and enjoy that her mere blonde presence made to every male in sight did not bely her nature. It was only through my firm insistence that she agreed to keep a prearranged appointment with her brother and his friends in Grafton Street. We taxied part of the way into town and arrived in the pub through separate entrances just in time to greet each other kindly, be swept off to the bona fides and back, eventually, to the house we had left, myself in a glow of physical and romantic satisfaction difficult to conceal.

Up to now, nice girl though she was to know, and keen pleasure to think of in the long day's dodging of Prunshios, what between associating with her friends and the general difficulty of pressing my suit, there had naturally been a good deal more effort than reward in the relationship. There were worse difficulties to come, but that evening was succeeded by an interval when she, as a woman should, took charge of our arrangements and made no reference to anything but the securing of secret hours of comradely enjoyment and an almost domestic peace. In her suburban bedroom, amid the signs and tokens of her femininity, and, I am bound to say, in the presence of a photograph of the late victim of the bona fide trade, I was often peacefully and happily loved.

Love. Am I wrong to blame all our subsequent difficulties on my altogether too free and frequent use of that word? I do not think so, though much, much too much, can certainly be attributed to the nonsensical enthusiasm with which I deployed it. But there were, in fact, difficulties outside my control. And there is nearly always a next step, which is nearly always beyond me. Anne, though not, I think, devout, was a native and a Catholic. The victim of the after-hours traffic in drink was but six months, if that, dead. He had left her nothing, not even what remained of the motor-car, for that had naturally belonged to the hire-purchase people. The brother who had charge of her was suitably concerned about Anne's reputation and anxious about her future. Put down my oddities to my literary avocations though he might, the sight of me cannot have been highly reassuring in either respect.

The interval of peace, lasting for perhaps two months and including many visits to the suburbs, was, I can now see, in the nature of an abandonment of struggle and forethought on Anne's part. We were now, in public, admittedly close friends, though not of course lovers. I took her to O'Turk's sometimes, but she insisted also on keeping up her social life, which meant going to the pubs and steak-houses with her steak-eating friends and their wives. If I wanted to see her on evenings when I was not paying a clandestine visit to the suburbs I had to venture into their company. When I did venture into it I could see that my unpopularity was bounding upwards.

Then Anne's own demeanour began to change. She was

as ready as ever to make assignations and they were as enjoyable, in their physical essentials, as before. But she wanted to talk. She wanted, I could see, for all her tact and fondness, to discuss the next step, to shift our relationship on to a different, and to her more satisfactory plane. I sympathised with her. Indeed I suffered for her, perhaps too much. We were now not only lovers, but allegedly in love. Our future togetherness was a matter of natural concern, apart altogether from whatever natural thoughts of the future Anne may have entertained. Yet, sympathise with her though I might, there seemed to me very little use, circumstanced as I was, in devoting any thought to the problem or, so far as was permitted me, in discussing it; and to fill, so to speak, the gap, I redoubled my protestations to the point where our relationship began to take on a slightly unreal, perhaps it is not too much to say, a hallucinatory, character. Though not highly literate, she had a sympathetic intelligence and perhaps much more unconventionality than even I presumed on, but my refusal to discuss practicalities of any kind, even extreme and unconventional solutions, had any such been possible, resembling as it did the stubborn incomprehension of the half-wit, gave her little chance to open her mind to me.

Then one evening, as we sat in the corner of a huge empty lounge in a pub in the Rathmines area, she told me about Joe. He had been a friend of the dear departed of bona fide fame. He was a member of the circle I had often been in, though I had scarcely noticed him. He was fond of her; he had said so. She had always known it. She liked him very much. She knew that only a delicacy arising from the fact that Jim was not many months dead and a respect for custom and propriety had prevented Joe from making more definite advances. It had been understood between them, and between herself and her brother, that in the course of time he would. She thought he knew she liked him, very much. He was very sweet. He was very upset at the moment because. Because what? Because he knows about us. Knows what? That we're friends and that I'm . . . fond of you. Oh well, to hell with him. But he was a friend of hers and had been of Jim's. She had known him for years. She was very fond of him. And in that great barn-like lounge, with its acres of red chairs and its purple and green neon tubing behind the bar, we drifted into our first quarrel.

I wronged her of course. She was trying to explain in what was really rather a touching way that she had crossed a rubicon for us. I accused her of lower and more obvious motives. We went from bad to worse. Shortly after this, though I do not think connected with it—it is more likely that she had been speaking to her confessor—there occurred a period of a month or so during which I was not allowed any clandestine visits to the suburbs at all. I moved out of "The Gurriers" and took a furnished room, a financial sacrifice of enormous size for which I yet received no credit, for neither would she visit me there. I began to rave back at Prunshios about the necessity for getting properly wurred in to life, hinting at all sorts of possibilities of true contact with the dialoctic if only I had more cash. Under extreme pressure he would sometimes part with a tenner and a blessing and rapidly changed the subject, but the occasions when I had the energy for this manoeuvre were so rare that it was obviously impossible to consider them as a means for supporting another human being, in respectability or otherwise.

At the beginning of this interregnum she made excuses about the sweet suburban assignations. Then she simply and obstinately said no. We met once or twice rather miserably in the gloomy empty lounges of Donnybrock and Rathmines. Further protestations seemed even worse than silence or making conversation. She went among her friends more often and I followed her, being swept now to the bona fides on a rising and, it was beginning to seem to me, rather dangerous tide of unpopularity. I became aware of Joe, a beefy, friendly auctioneer, with, like Tennyson, in spite of his broken heart, many anecdotes. I could see she encouraged him to believe that all was not lost, how disingenuously or merely femininely I did not know. Her bereavement was now considered sufficiently remote for her to attend functions of a social order and I knew she went to golf-club dances and the like of that with him, the brother and a rather nasty female friend of her brother's. He also escorted her to the theatre. They were none of them without slight cultural pretensions.

Then there occurred a period of greater friendliness and meetings both in the suburbs and in my room, the upkeep of which was crippling my activities all round. The brother spoke to me, politely but obscurely, about our relationship and her friends spoke, I guessed, rather less obscurely to her. My inability to put up rounds when in their company had damned me in their eyes as a fitting associate for Anne. Rumours were circulating about us, and both her reputation and her future prospects were being damaged irreparably. I, who when considering, in my desultory and impractical way, the forms of relationship with the opposite sex available and practical for one circumstanced and situated as I was, had been dubious about adultery, was now being made to feel like several treacherous adulterers rolled into one, a callous wrecker of lives and happiness on a monstrous scale. I had sought compromise and peace, but peace was denied me. I am not precisely an immoralist. I tend, in my limited way, to worry about the effects my frequently disastrous behaviour is having on other people, generally in the very small hours when no reparation is possible, and I was consumed now with guilt. I shambled, with guilt at my heels, down those staring concrete roadways with the few wind-torn bushes fighting for a foothold in the imperfectly reclaimed and newly fenced gardens. All my fear of the suburbs had returned and when I stepped off the bus into the eerie semi-silence of concrete villadom I knew myself an alien and a stranger. As for my room, with its frayed linoleum, its single upright chair, its gas-fire and pink bed coverlet, it was enough to knock the steam out of the most insensitive of girls, and Anne was never that. She tried to do small things with it, but her heart was not in it; indeed it was beginning to be all too terribly plain to us both that except at odd moments our hearts were no longer fully in the whole thing, that the pressures were too strong and the guilts and unspoken differences too great.

And when I speak of pressures I mean what I say. There were beginning to be small demonstrations against me in the pubs and at parties, outbreaks that stopped barely short of violence, an unmistakable and possibly soon uncontrollable popular clamour. Yet, more especially as the gulf between us and our private communication grew more and more imperfect, I could not keep away from them. They were a large circle, composing, as it sometimes seemed to me, the entire population of several pubs, and I did not seem able to avoid meeting them, and forcing myself on them, whether they had Anne with them or not. If she was with them I joined them out of some obscure principle; sometimes because she and I were then on terms of intimacy; often, for we had now reached a stage not of quarrels and reconciliations so much as of silent driftings apart and taciturn comings together, because we were not; and I desired to be again. If I avoided their pubs, I frequently met up with them in the bona fides and it seems to me that I joined them recklessly, whether she was there or not, for some reason that I cannot bear to examine. Thus my reputation as an imbiber of free drink grew along with whatever other reputations I may have had. I was losing touch with other associates and becoming a mere, barely tolerated, hanger-on of the bourgeoisie. The situation was ridiculous. Added to my guilt there were the hangovers accruing from such a circle of acquaintance; the suffering of insult, intended or not; the idiotic conversations enthusiastically engaged in. And there was the poison in our relationship itself when we had any, the dodging of the question of the next step. I tried to make it unspokenly clear that I would have been glad to have settled down with her in some place of our own had she possessed the cash, or the job, or the mastery of circumstance, or contempt for public opinion that were necessary, but that she did not and except for the last item neither did I, but this, instead of getting said, got mixed up with my protestations. My unhappiness on this score was real enough, but I am bound to say it was nothing to the agonies I was beginning to experience out of confusion of motive, self-questioning, disgust at those protestations, sheer guilt.

Looking back on it now I can see that with a very little effort, even within the limits of action available, I could have managed the whole thing better. I could have made her feel better at least by regularising our relationship on an intellectual plane and bringing the arts and the artistic temperament into the matter, for she would have been impressed by their penumbra and enjoyed being taken to the theatre, introduced to actors, and welcomed into literary society. It is possible that these gambits, if I had performed them enthusiastically enough, might have given our connection an entirely different character; and, in that conjunction of others' eyes and their own which is always important to women, would have blessed it with the latitude of art and conferred upon it the prestige of an intellectually grounded passion, notions to which women are susceptible as soon as they pass beyond the very first degrees of literacy.

But I sweated and twitched in the theatre, from drought, anxiety and boredom; loathed such actors as I knew; and, in spite of my status as editor, was not well-received in such literary society as I had ever met. As I shall have occasion to explain, my acquaintance in that direction was limited, with the exception of O'Turk's; and O'Turk's, as pubs will from time to time, was passing through a bad period, and would scarcely have passed the most ignorant eye as a simulacrum of the world of art. The company of such disconsolate gurriers and beggars as were then to be found there, or the occasional aloof Japanese, was, I am afraid, scarcely such as to give an illusion of daring, distinction and poetic fervour to our or any other affairs of the heart. Besides, my activities on *The Trumpet* and failure to get their works past Prunshios, were alienating such semi-literary companions as I had ever had.

Still, I might have done better in terms of assuaging the disquiet which she very naturally felt. I could, with some measure of honesty I suppose, have at least invoked or suggested the gloomy, introverted, tortured poet. But the persona I adopted was a confused and unsatisfactory one; and, as it was, through some obstacle in my nature, and some obstacle not entirely divorced from cash surrounding the whole matter, I played straight into the hands of the enemy, and became a mere free-loader in the circle she inhabited, instead of drawing her into any I might have created for myself.

WHAT wonder then, between one thing and another, that the precise shade of social optimism, the ability to see one's private affairs as part of a general pattern, to take one's place in the life of the community, that Prunshios tirelessly demanded of me was difficult; or that what enthusiasm I had ever felt for Associating with the Editor had, like my enthusiasm for Assisting the Secretary long ago, fallen to a low ebb. What my private problems, as extraordinary and as peripheral as ever, had to do with the dialoctic I really did not know.

Nor, to tell you the truth, did I find it easy to concentrate on my work with Casey's monologue, compounded as it was of the most awful prognoses, forebodings and warnings, continually ringing in my ears. I was compelled to avoid the office, like Casey himself, for much of the day because of the presence, or putative presence of Prunshios, for he had taken to going there more often. We used to meet in the bookmaker's, or the pub around the corner, and discuss the likelihood, or the the imminent likelihood, of his presence, according to a species of bush-lore which Casey had acquired through the years, a lore which was partly mystic divination and partly empirical science, involving actual observation from the window of the pub, spurious phone-calls to Prunshios' residence, interviews with the car-park attendant in O'Connell Street, examination of the blotter on the desk, as well as more arcane means of divination, to do with Casey's dreams and visions. The result of our mutual avoidance of the third party, however, was that the time we both did actually spend in the office, which consisted of a single small room, tended to overlap, and to be given over mostly to Casey's commentaries.

"Whatever the hell he was up to there, I'd lay it went astray on him. I wouldn't be one bit surprised but he nearly over-reached himself that time, the terrible humour he's in, never out of the office, my God up and down the stairs like a funicular railway. He has my nerves gone so bad on me I don't know whether I'm imaginin' things. You know when you're associatin' with that fellow you get to thinkin' the whole world is up to some hookey business or other. Did you see where the Northern Correspondent napped that winner of Fallaps's yesterday? Oh he's in bad straits at the moment, I can see that, and that's the time to watch out. There was a letter here this mornin' I swear it was from a money-lender, anyway whatever the hell was in it, he was scowlin' and roarin' under his breath, I couldn't get a civil word out of him. I swear to God I've known that fellow thirty or forty years and not a civil word could I get out of him. Then on with the hat and off to hell with him out of here. We're safe now anyway, we won't see him for the rest of the day, he'll be gallivantin' around the town like a mad thing tryin' to stave off calamity."

Thus, leaning over the back of his chair, he would continue to occupy our master's time, giving an odd hitch to the skirts of the overcoat which he wore perpetually to give substance, when surprised, to the assertion that he was just on his way out to see about an advertisement or an account.

"And do you know something? Associating with that fellow is a very, very dangerous game. I could tell you stories. Oh, I could tell you. A trail of dead men. There were three men in a cell with that fellow and they were taken out one after the other and shot, while his gills was left there sayin' his prayers. And only last year there was Bill McMurphy—sure you read it all in the papers but that fellow's name was kept out of it—the time of the Mayo Linen Company business. He was in that up to his oxters. Seven years poor McMurphy got, as decent a man as ever pulled on a shoe, and that fellow came in here to the office that same morning whistlin'. Whistlin'. He doesn't care, Paddy. He does not care. He's ruthless. And he's very, very dangerous. He may bear a charmed life himself—though by God I think he must be very near the edge this time from the black look of him—but you want to look out for yourself if you have any dealings with that ould bollocks. It's not today nor yesterday I discovered the grim truth of that."

Then, after the man, I would have the master. I would be trapped suddenly in the office perhaps, when the signs and portents had proved false, or compelled for mere decency's sake at long last to accede to a meeting, for Prunshios' main delight lay in delivering himself in the coffays of injunctions and saws and maxims and warnings, in measuring the extent of my social extroversion, my progress or backsliding, and in flattering himself shamelessly and endlessly through reminiscence and anecdote which showed that when young he had had the virtues of youth, and that now that he was getting on a bit he had the wisdom of age, each story ending in a saw or a folk-saying or a pithy moral about the way to fight the good fight and a clear implication that I and my generation were lacking in this or that. I do not know whether he realised the effect these conversations were having on my nerves. Far more surely than relaxing drugs would have done, they were driving me towards the *déreglement de tous les sens*, towards a complete inability to distinguish a movement of the dialoctic from a tram plunging down Dawson Street. On me, and on the magazine equally, he was having precisely the opposite of the bracing effect superficially intended, but then he enjoyed the occasions so much that I don't supposed he cared.

Patriotic hat in hand, fine head bared to the spring sunshine, his step lightened by the prospect of an hour or two's torture, he would stride across O'Connell Street to the coffay, while I slunk or shambled or shuffled or tottered behind him, my mind darkening as we went.

"I'm not entirely hoppy about you, Paddy," he would declare, once cakes and coffee had been set before us. "It seems to me you're waverin' on the road. Ye hove an opportunity now to strike a spark that the fresh gale of yer mind would blow into a flame that might transform the whole country, but yer turned inward. Yer emanatin' unhoppiness. Doubts are all very well, but we've had enough of unhoppiness. The lads that are writin' now will be lookin' to you for leadership, not for self-onolysis. That's not what the objoctive situation demands."

Who were these lads? The majority of the "yong"—the word obsessed Prunshios—writers I knew were the Japanese or American *rentiers* who commuted between Dublin and Paris, the limeys or the O'Turk's beggars. Sometimes the Japanese or Americans abandoned a girl in

Dublin, to be devoured by the girl-hungry locals; occasionally they could be touched for small sums; but their knowledge of peasants and fishermen was limited to the Japanese or Californian variety and their writing when it existed at all could scarcely be called constructive. On the few occasions when I produced small works of theirs for his inspection, Prunshios waved them aside indignantly. Indeed nothing that these classes produced, on the rare occasions when they produced anything at all, impressed him whatever. Something, an obession with geography or herrings or the acrobatics of the dialoctic was absent.

In quiet desperation I made an inventory of all the native writers remaining in the country. I found that these were almost without exception employed in the radio-station, a large and gloomy building in the principal street, where they occupied positions varying in importance from that of doorkeeper to that of director, depending on the number of novels they had published and the orthodoxy of their religious views. I consulted one whom I knew, an atheist who had once written a short-story and now had a permanent and pensionable post in the radio station as a lavatory attendant. After some consideration he arranged a meeting in a pub for me with a dramatist who had once had a one-act play performed at the Abbey, but who had signed a letter of protest when a schoolteacher of mildly heretical views had been stoned to death by a mob urged on by the Bishop of Ballyhamnis. This man had some sort of a job on the roof of the radio-station, something to do with flag-poles, I think, or lightning conductors, in any case he was up there in all weathers and it seemed to drain him of his energies, and though he offered to introduce me to the Protestant essayist who, he said, operated the ventilating system, or was perhaps assistant to the operator of the ventilating system, the whole thing came to nothing, for a complex of reasons.

On the perhaps unwarrantable assumption that they were closer to geography and the dialoctic than my Japanese friends, I would gladly have filled the whole magazine with the flag-pole man, the lavatory attendant and the assistant to the ventilating system, but for one thing they exhibited a marked reluctance to write, perhaps fearing promotion, for near the top competition was said to be especially keen, and a man had to attend mass on weekdays and publish at least one peasant novel every four years if he was to keep his job. For another, and this seemed to me, even, rather odd, though Prunshios stormed on about the "yong", he seemed when it came down to practical preferences, to be heavily biased in favour of the compositions of their elders. Though not exactly in the first blush of youth, the flag-pole man and his friends were at least a little less hoary than their superiors in religion, yet it was these latter that Prunshios seemed definitely to prefer; and he tirelessly held them up as examples to all beneath the age of forty; and pointed to their senile contributions, which he introduced independently into the magazine, as exactly what the dialoctic ordered.

One day, instead of taking me to the coffay for a pep-talk, he took me to see an eminent man in the gloomy building, his friend McMurkagaun, the religious novelist. I knew of this individual slightly by reputation and of late I had been hearing a great deal of him from Prunshios. My friend the flag-pole man had also told me about him. Even at the top, where mysticism was common, he was acknowledged to have special insights into the mysteries of religion, though it was said also that one would never guess this from the down to earth friendliness of his manner, and that devout though he might be, he was a common man like ourselves and as much or more so afflicted with the temptations of the flesh. I had never read his books, but I remembered hearing it said by a Gaelic speaking intellectual of my acquaintance that they were "strong stuff". The faith triumphed, but the operations of grace were cruel. The schoolteacher's passion for the agricultural inspector's wife almost overthrows his soul. In utmost clarity of vision he chooses sin and damnation, but grace operates in some terrible way, a road accident or something like that, and though he rages against the lash he is saved in the end. At least that is how I imagined the books from what I heard, as belonging, in fact, to a harmless but tedious school of the day.

We walked, Prunshios and I, through the long corridors chanting McMurkagaun's praises, and eventually we were ushered into the presence of the man himself. He was sitting behind a big desk smoking a pipe and beaming. He looked like several common men rolled into one: cattle jobber, schoolmaster, politician, publican, Knight of Columbanus, member of the Gaelic League. He might have been through the dark night of the soul, he might have come near the edge of the abyss, he might even have seen visions, and he had certainly written a round dozen of novels, but he was putting on no side. God and Gaelic civilisation, I could see, were for everyone.

"Well, and well, and well, Prunshios," he said in a softly-nurtured Kerry accent as he rose to greet us, "and is it yourself, your venerable but sprightly self that's paying us a visit. Well 'tis you should know how welcome you are, anyway, and we on our bended knees to you every day in the week to come in here and use our microphones. We have several, you know, most of them in working order." He lowered his waggish finger and turned to me. "But did I hear a whisper on the telephone about another visitor, a certain young spalpeen who's telling us oldsters in a certain magazine that we'd better look out, one of the young intellectuals that I keep hearing so much about but find it so difficult to meet?" His expression of quizzical severity was suddenly replaced by bland good humour. He held out his hand. "Sit down, Paddy, sit down and take your ease. I've heard a great deal about you. You're as well known to me as . . . as I am to you. And, though you may not believe it, you're among friends here." He turned to Prunshios. "So this is your live wire, eh? This is the new age and the new witness. Once again"—he raised chubby, strong schoolmaster's hands expansively, twinkling from one to the other—"once again the voice of the young is heard, masking its hurt in its anger, disowning the generation that went before, proclaiming a scorched earth policy, telling us all to go and bury our fat heads, what? And very fine too. Very fine and proper and usual. Oh, it's not so long since I was young myself, Paddy—not so long if he'll permit me, as it is since Prunshios was, anyway, though that, mind you, is according to the record book, for I've a sneaking suspicion that according to another reckoning he might turn out to be the youngest of us all. What, you old fire-eater, do you find you're still younger, and angrier, than the youngest and the angriest of them? But to get back to what I was saying Paddy. The generations revolt, each in their own time, and it would be a worse world, or at least a duller world—and the world you know is better seen comically than tragically as long as God in his mercy gives us the choice—if that weren't the case. All right, you young intellectuals are in revolt. You're bitter. You're angry and you say so. But I wonder could you answer me one question, now that we're here face to face?"

I was prepared to be of any help I could in anything, if only to put an end to these endless references to my non-existent nonage, references which made me feel more wretched and decrepit than ever, and which I could not but persist in thinking, in spite of all the evidence to the contrary, were somehow meant sarcastically and as an insult to my care-worn and unlaurelled brow. But I was stunned. Apart from some wretched, defeatist maunderings written at Prunshios's stern behest I had uttered no word of protest about anything. On what was this fantasy, so, as I was only beginning to realise, prevalent among the geographers when they came to the topic of age, based? What did this offensive man wish me to say?

"Do you think you could answer me, Paddy, now that I've had the pleasure, and it is a pleasure, of meeting you face to face, one simple question about the young intellectuals of today?"

I could not. I did not, for a start, know who he was referring to, or indeed what he was talking about, but he had me and he knew it.

"Why is it, Paddy, that your generation—I'm not speaking about you all now, I'm not one to generalise—but about what I think we may say is a very vocal section, conducts its controversies without reference to the deep, God-given, basic verities of existence? Don't get me wrong, now, don't get me wrong. I have uttered my protest in my time, when I was younger, and maybe, for all we know, wiser. Those great men Gilbert Chesterton and Hilaire Belloc spent their rampageous lives in controversy. But it was all with reference to the facts, Paddy, to the dung out of which we've all grown, to . . . to sex, and birth, and hunger, men and women and the soil, to . . . dirt and ordure and the laughter that comes out of a man's belly when the gaiety of ultimate desperation lifts him above despair. Your generation, Paddy, if you'll forgive me saying so, gives me the impression that you know nothing about these things. You're . . . you're abstract, doctrinaire, intellectual, arid, you're the generation of Eliot and I. A. Richards and that lot. Better, Paddy, spend your life with toss-pots than with intellectuals. Contemplate the beggarman, Paddy, there's more wisdom in him than in all your barren, cosmopolitan smart-alecs. Here in Ireland, Paddy, we're lucky, we still have the noble and the beggarman, we can feel the throb of life in the desperado, the thief and the buckeen with an eye for the girls. My God, Paddy, I've learned more from taking a bundle of a girl in my arms and thumping it to a melodeon on a Saturday night with the yellow ale inside me than I could from all your existentialists put together. And then, Paddy, and then when you come to controversy, you come with the wisdom of the ditches and the sheebeens, which is more ancient and wiser and more like the wisdom of God than anything you'll find in the universities and the schools of thought that your generation appears to frequent."

He beamed upon me once more, victorious but magnanimous, and I beamed back as best I could, unable, as so often, to begin at the beginning. But Prunshios was boiling for a word.

"Well, now Seumas," he began, leaning cheerfully back in his chair, his hat dangling to the floor. "What you say is onteresting. And I'll go further. It's percoptive. But there may be another sonse in which it is just wan wee mite superfocial. In fact if you'll take an old mon's word for it, there is a sonse in which like mony of the yong fellas of today, you're talking through your hot. You're half-way right, of course, about the goneration that Paddy here belongs to. Paddy would be better off maybe livin' in a slum and learning what it is to go hungry now and then. As far as drinking is concorned I don't approve of it myself. I've seen the harm it did to the social struggle. But I will say this. If he does go drinking, it would be better to do it in an extrovort than in an introvort fashion. There's too much concontration on unhoppiness among the yong of today. And thot's barren. Thot's barren I will admit. I mean personal unhoppiness, not the unhoppiness thot's caused by the social structure. And you're right too about the foct thot they've lost touch with the grond buck-leppin', dovil-may care gaiety of Ireland. I don't approve of drinking, mind you. I don't approve of drinking. But I like to see the blood racin' in a yong fella's veins. He'd be better off maybe slutherin' a young widda in a ditch thon readin' Richardson ond Ellis ond the like of those yong fellas you were talkin' about. You and I are not ontellectuals in the sense thot these yong fellas are ontellectuals. But thot doesn't say thot ontellectualism is always wrong. Not if it's wurred in to the prosent historical situation. You and I are men who in our way are wurred in to living. You hove your job and yer home where you live among people who onderstond the reolities of living—in however confused a way, mind you, but thot doesn't motter, you con interprot them. I've been involved in the social struggle all my life. I've often been wrong, mind you, I won't dispute it, but I've tried to understond the dialoctic and what it demonded at ony given moment. Now the fault I find with Paddy's ontellectualities. . . ."

And so they relaxed, talking their remote and contradictory jargon, while the object of their discourse and their diagnoses discomposed in his chair. They both, I knew, led lives of the utmost decency and surburban propriety. However fond of a flutter Prunshios might be, and whatever nefarious dealings he might engage in with his respectable regime friends, his private life, like that of the fat man opposite him, was quiet to the point of monotony, the climax of an evening being the rosary with the head buried in the chair. Why were they urging breaches of the natural and moral law on me?

I awoke from these reflections to hear them discussing, those two grown men, the prospects of a symposium on their respective positions by the "younger generation" and their elders, to be captained by McMurkagaun. They appeared not to hear my protests.

"In all modesty, Paddy," said the mystic, his pipe now between his teeth, his expression severe but friendly, "I feel I'm the man for the job. You see the question of whether I was young or old has never interested me. I feel that a young man who's concerned with his age is proving himself to be without the capacity for being swept away by the tides of youth, the tides in the hot blood that are maybe a simulacrum of eternity. There's the business of ordinary living of course, Paddy, as no doubt you'll discover, getting married, settling down, making your way, establishing yourself, doing the best job you can when maybe you don't feel like doing it, these things remind a man of his age in time; but they're only the pattern of the dance, within which the blood is still leaping. Read Peguy, Paddy," he said, rising and offering me one Gaelic palm. "Close your Sartres's and your Camus's and open your Peguy."

"The vory mon for the job, Paddy," said Prunshios as he strode bareheaded down the corridors, myself trotting behind. "He'll treat what ye hove to say gently, but he'll treat it fairly too. It'll be good for you yong fellows to hove a rousin', stand-up discussion with an ontellect like McMurkagaun's. I often think that what's wrong with the lot of you is that you don't expose your subjoctive states and your subjoctive pains to thot kind of hard, bony onolysis. Even if you could elevate yer subjoctive feelings, which I doubt, to the level of thesis, there hos to be ontithesis. Get a good team together now this time, a good crowd of lively, alert, darin' and gay yong fellows. But responsible, responsible. Ond Irish, not like some of thot gang you've been showin' me lately. The problem hos to be discussed in the context of our present situation." He waved his patriotic hat at the spring sunshine, the trams, the ice-cream parlours and an afternoon cinema queue. "Here and now. Come along to the coffay now and we'll hove a chat. Yer doin' fine. Yer doin' fine. But yer maybe not as alort as ye should be to the dangers of confusin' yer more personal difficulties and emotions with what Life" —he waved his hat again—"is thinkin' and doin' indepondently of ye just now. We couldn't hove a better mon for this job than Seumas. He'll be fair to you. But he'll take no nonsense. There's clay on his boots. He thinks in the bone. It'll do ye good, it'll do ye all good. Even if what he hos to say hurts you, it'll not harm you in the latter ond, not if yer monly enough. But we'll talk about thot in the coffay. Is there anything yer short or before we go in? I'm not sure if ye con get cigarottes or onything like that in this place. Here's a ten-bob note. Go and get yerself some cigarettes ond I'll order some cakes for ye inside."

In the betting shop whither I immediately repaired with the ten-bob note, I met Casey. "He's as thick as two thieves with that cunt McMurkagaun. I wonder what the hell they're up to together. Damn all to do with *The Trumpet* anyway, I'd lay. And by God if I was McMurkagaun I'd look out for myself. There's few that get's entangled with bollocky bill that escapes unscathed. I can't make out what the hell Fallaps is doin' this weather at all. And I see where the Scout gives the next one, n.b. That bollocks has me so bewildered I can't put two and two together at all."

SPRING became summer. The tulips and the girls flowered in Stephen's Green; the sunlight reached into the furthest corners of the pubs, revealing figures that had slumbered there unnoticed through the long winter. Twilight would come gently to Grafton Street; the summer darkness arrived with closing time and afterwards the bona fides blazed on the mountains; the noise of strong men swearing eternal fealty and eternal enmity being heard in the deserted city like the rumour of a hostile army, the back-slapping like small-arms fire in the larger noise. At ten o'clock the cars swept out along the mountain roads as if all those who could muster transport were fleeing before a plague; at half-past twelve they swept back, awash with song and Guinness, as if the defences of Dublin had suddenly crumbled before a mechanised, drunken horde; and from then until dawn the noise of breaking glass, of splintering wood and cracking skulls would float out over the warm and star-dappled waters of the bay.

Summer became graced with the first autumnal tints. But I had no zest for the delights of either season. Though outward bound and inward bound I would cling precariously to fender and running board, or be squashed high near the roof on the outward run and trampled under foot on the return, the responsibilities of associating with an editor were weighing me down. Besides, matters with Anne had gone from bad to worse. I was now in the ridiculous position of a man who protested everything and circumstantially accomplished nothing. Far from Orpheus being able to draw her with his lute from the confines in which she was trapped, he appeared in the ludicrous role of one who hung about taking illegally and deceitfully what he could, including the free drink of her companions in the nether world, while rampaging at the same time about the extent and power of his passion.

And as the monsoon season broke on the fair isle, Prunshios, perhaps because he had in fact over-reached himself at last, grew ever more exhausting in his demands. As far as I was concerned, at least, Casey's dire prophesies about the penalties of association with him looked like coming true. The wretched symposium had materialised at last, but what my contribution to it cost me, in expense of spirit, in wastage of shame, I dread even now to think. To allow the word young to be used of one; to use it oneself, as if unblushingly; to flounder in the geographers' terminology, as if one cared; to be induced to play the role of member of a generation in order that the fiction might be maintained that something of public importance happened in the wretched place every so many years: all this agony, for God only knows what reason, I endured.

"A fine lot of young writers," McMurkagaun's contribution had begun, "A fine lot of spalpeen fanachs come tottering on the crutches of the word young as if youth were an infirmity for which they were much to be pitied instead of a racing, coursing tide in the reckless blood. . . ."

I began to see that the whole thing was a biological necessity to the geographers, without which they feared that they would vanish, patriotic hats, black coats and all, through lack of the necessary onti-thesis.

I sank rapidly, I don't deny it, and that awful symposium marked a definite stage in my downfall. Though I had moved out of "The Gurriers", and now had a room of sorts, my health continued to decline. My piles, my athlete's foot, my chronic catarrh had returned. Meanwhile, maddened by the dialoctic, goaded into frenzied action in the coffays by a sudden onset of creditors, a mass seizure of sweep tickets by the English police or an outburst of hooliganism involving the defacement of large quantities of rubbish baskets, Prunshios raved and gnashed about inshore fishery, the younger generation and the necessity to convert potatoes into electricity. A scheme for paving the streets of Dublin with sods of turf obsessed him, and he insisted on writing editorials about it, printing them cheek by jowl with articles on Heidegger by the Japanese and a controversy about Jansenism which his friends from the radio-station, concerned as always with degrees of orthodoxy, were somehow conducting in our columns. The editor of *Furthest Horizons*, the highbrow magazine in whose pages I had formerly appeared, shouted rude jokes about carrigeen moss and dried herrings at me as he drove past with the Japanese and their girls in his large American car; acquaintances who knew me only in my other persona murmured audibly about articles entitled "Cork Literature: Is It Dead?" or the "The Genius of Seumas McMurkagaun". I was under pressure from all fronts. I was breaking up, and I knew it. I sat so long in the coffays that I had taken to drinking the stuff and was suffering, as I now see, from an advanced form of what the Americans have since diagnosed as coffee-nerves; a little more and I might have become the founder of the hop-head school, seen visions, declared myself, if not positively God, at least a minor prophet, but even that was denied me. Prunshios had taken to consorting with a new peasant writer, an enormous oaf with sea-boots, a Kerry accent and a pioneer pin, and I was subjected to his diagnoses also in the coffays where we made a curious trio, two all tweed and extroversion, myself giving more and more point to their repeatedly expressed warnings about the dangers of subjectivity. I did not mind printing this sycophant, indeed at that stage I did not mind printing anybody, but I objected to his accent, his conversation and his sneers. At length I ceased to take any part in the discussions, but I had to sit there while they shook their heads over me and mouthed about the dialoctic. I could see this fellow was after my job.

One day towards the end of autumn, when the leaves had fallen in Baggot Street and the girls had disappeared from Stephen's Green, Prunshios summoned me to the most palatial of his coffays, ordered me a plate of cakes and pronounced my doom.

"A mon of your tolents is wasted as an oditor," he declared with conviction. "The place for a poet is with the masses. Yer too sheltered. Ye should let the fresh wund of yer mind blow on something else. Immerse yerself in the dialoctic. Take a close look at the life of the people. Do you know what the forward-looking elements are doing at the moment? They're omigrating. It's a necessary part of the historical process. Go to England," he shouted, so loudly that a parish priest woke up at a neighbouring table and an elderly waitress looked at us with nun-like disapproval.

He pulled out his wad and peeled off four tenners. "Go to England and live in a doss-house. The prosent dialoctical situation con only be understood in the doss-houses of London."

He grabbed his hat and his bill. "Finish yer cakes. Finish yer cakes," he cried, working his way to the door, slapping elderly clerics absent-mindedly on the shoulders. At the desk he turned.

"Trust yerself to the dialoctic," he cried, his hat in the air. "Go to England and live in a doss-house. . . ."

It was the wrong time of year for the movement of peoples, but I took his advice. That evening, as the gulls dipped and swept and cried over the greying waters of the Liffey, I stood at the rail of the cattle-boat and gazed mournfully at the mountainsides where soon the bonas would be blazing and, for all I knew, Anne would be responding, almost unnoticeably, but softly and maddeningly, to the good Joe's manful efforts to please. I had not said good-bye. My heart, though suitably melancholy, was not exactly heavy. There are situations which are best brought lightly to a close.

Next morning, in the blearier grey of a Liverpool dawn, I hopped a lorry to London and, I devoutly hoped, a quietly satisfactory relationship with the dialoctic. Much has been made of the metaphysics of the hitch-hike since those days; whole schools of writing devoted solely to the cosmic significance of the free-lift have swept continents. Industrious old men who had never thumbed their way anywhere have gone cursing to their graves because they found themselves, not for the first time, devoid of the fashionable material of the day. But this was before the time of the beats, and, so far as I know, nobody attached any particular spiritual importance to the cadging of lifts at all.

At the entrance to the tunnel a tired, taciturn, grimy and monosyllabic man received me into the cab of his eight-wheeler and in answer to my question muttered something reassuring about "the smoke". The day that dawned on us as we banged southward through the tangle of brickwork, wheels, towers, chimneys and giant heaps of plain dirt that the industrial revolution has bequeathed to its first love, was touched with the remote, golden sunshine of late autumn. My companion demanded no conversation. Our conveyance shared the road on terms of equality with tankers, huge wagons with tarpaulin trailers swishing along behind, fore-and-afters with whole suspension bridges slung in the middle; and we towered above everything else. For mile after soothing and surrealist mile we swopped Woodbines and an occasional grunt. When we stopped at a transport café towards midday we were getting along so well that he insisted on paying for the meat and two veg. I had come this way more than once before, and was to come it often enough again, but rarely so happily as on that autumn day. I was leaving a hell of a lot behind.

True to his word, my companion was bound for the smoke, and we hit it before dark. As commanded by Prunshios I went straight to a doss-house in Camden Town, a large and gloomy building which reminded me a little of the Dublin radio station.

Fog hung perpetually in the corridors, which extended for miles and resounded by night and day with shouts of "Ashtowk Paddy!" "I'll sphplit the bashtard", "Come up, Mick!", "By Jasus I'll ate 'im", "I'm after buryin' the mother", "Puck him, Christy" and other such pleasantries. The Irish were there in force and the dialoctic was in full swing; indeed it was all that the small group of harassed English officials who ran the place could do to prevent it getting out of hand altogether; it took all the immense pseudo-moral authority of the English lower middle classes to prevent large-scale massacre on Saturday nights.

Taking it altogether though, I thought that, if this was the true dialoctic at last, it was a rest after Prunshios. One had a cubicle and a bed and a chamber pot. There was a canteen which was comparatively safe, for the Irish scorned to eat; and there was a television room which was altogether safe, for the ranks of third Ypres veterans who sat there in caps and mufflers would, it was tacitly understood, have torn the Irish apart had they dared to intrude upon the most precious of a pensioner's remaining pleasures. It was true that the fog hung thick between one and the screen; but this was England after all; the illusion of reality was, if anything, increased, as on the afternoon when the pensioners and I witnessed (if that is the word) the Manchester November Handicap run in a thick fog at Manchester through a thick fog in the Rowton.

I spent many pleasant hours in the fog among the pensioners, silent except for an occasional toothless cackle, or an even more occasional, "good, in't 'e?", a question to which it was only necessary to reply by shifting a little in one's wooden chair, and still remember with gratitude the fog-bedimmed features of many of the popular idols of the day, now alas departed to whatever unpublicised bourne awaits such comparatively nice people.

If in the canteen and the telly room one was safe among the English, the Welsh, the Scots, and the Geordies, the hallways, and particularly the entrance hall, were given over to the sister island. It was dangerous to hold a bloodshot glance for more than a fraction of a second, and even the most scornful, independent, indigenous, capped and muffiered of pensioners was inclined on occasion to hasten his step. One's nerves grew frayed in time, so that a single roar of "Ashtowk Paddy!" was inclined to make one jump; the noise of hobnailed boots tramping down a corridor to make one quake with a sort of unreasoning terror. Apart from the fog, and the hawking and spitting, the stink of urine doing battle with disinfectant and the dangers represented by my compatriots, the place was restful, comfortable, even salubrious; nor was there any need to stir beyond its precincts for most of the bare necessities of life, which is a great advantage in any establishment. One had to get up at a frosty hour it is true, when the corridors were invaded by squads of hearty old women whose job it was to turn the residents out of the sheets, empty the chamber pots into gigantic buckets, make the beds and sweep up the blood and vomit; there was a little too much of the public lavatory about the interior decoration of the building; and in the perpetual murk it was impossible to read, even if there had been any place but the telly room adapted to the pursuits of leisure; yet restful, in a sense, it was. Nonetheless, facts had to be faced. Prunshios' bounty was running out. The faculty of eyesight might quite possibly atrophy.

It is in such circumstances that the demons of action arise to tear one's remaining shreds of peace apart. When I had ten shillings left I had the, probably illusory, notion that I would have to act; that I needed a background of operations, a world in which to move. My monastic life in the Rowton was, I told myself, like most monastic immolations, purely self-indulgent; besides, it would come to an end. I would starve, or die of exposure; and I had a duty not to starve, or die of exposure. To whom did I owe this duty? Certainly not to myself, for I would have been happy enough to run the venture. And it can hardly have been to anybody else. O obscure and fraudulent moral imperatives, how you mock us. And, if it comes to that, how you mocked me continually, drove me in fact nearly demented, during the next stage of my career.

Goaded by the demons of action I recollected that I had a friend called Coosins to whom I had once, in a moment of illusory prosperity, lent five pounds; that he worked in, or about, or for the B.B.C.; and I felt compelled to ring him up.

HOW shall I describe Coosins to those who are not acquainted with his ilk, with the organisation which provides him with perhaps the only environment in which his talents, so numerous and yet so evanescent, so real and yet so difficult of definition, could flourish? The voice on the telephone is a mixture of joy, joviality, concern, affection and remorse. The Irishisms are accurately phrased, even sometimes in the matter of phrasing, improved upon, yet slightly inaccurately employed.

"Ashtowk Paddy, and how could ye be so long in the big, big city, and you leavin' me here without sight nor sound of you even on the telephone itself? Now whisht down a minnit till I tell you. I'm after havin' a drink on

Monday when it will be a week from last Monday if you follow my drift in a great big public housh with some very impowrtant people from the stance of gettin' you a job, or maybe, for the matter of that, two jobs to do in the great big B.B.C., so why don't you come along and dry up your whistle along with us? Now wait there a minnit till I'll be gosterin' to you where it is. . . ."

It is no easy matter either to describe the feelings of a man who has lived, as I had done, monastically, in an enclosed community, for some weeks, and who at length emerging; and proceeding into, literally, the only other building he has entered for those weeks, is confronted not with the entirely different community he expects, but with one which appears to be identical with the one he has just left. Imagine the curious surrealist shock I experienced, when at length I pushed open the door of the Stork, to find it ringing with cries of "Ashtowk Paddy!", "Come up, Mick", "I'm after buryin' the mother", yes and even, "Puck him, Christy", "I'll shplit the bashtard" and "By Jasus I'll ate 'im".

I retreated for a moment, terror-struck, fearful on the one hand for my sanity, and on the other that I who had survived so long with the pensioners in the Rowton might now become the victim in, of all places, a B.B.C. pub of a misdirected hob-nailed boot. My fears, as I stood half in and half out of the swing door, were at length quelled, not only by the sight of Coosins himself among a group in one corner, but by the air of indubitable joviality, indeed benignity, with which these cries were uttered. The language might be the same, but the dialoctic was undoubtedly different. I pushed the door fully open and entered not only the pub but a curious interregnum in my existence, if indeed my existence, which is undoubtedly in one sense an interregnum itself, can be said to contain separate interregnums within it.

The group among which Coosins stood proclaimed their loyalty to the ould sod by the tweediness of their talk, no less than by the tweeds they wore. That the sod in their case was mostly the black north; that every last man jack of them was Protestant to the back teeth, hindered their enthusiasm not at all. Indeed as I grew, in the succeeding months, more closely acquainted with them, I was to discover that so far from hampering their style, or bringing a blush of shame to their cheeks, their membership of the traditionally oppressing class seemed to drive them on to a veritable frenzy, a sort of dervish dance of Irishry, which was to me a wonder to behold.

The celticism of their speech sometimes resulted in a strange incoherence, not to say raving. The effect was of delirium. Among those to whom Coosins introduced me was a former Belfast barrister called Boddells, a poet whose heavily alliterative verse was known to me from the anthologies. He was the most extreme. He spoke in gnomic pseudo-proverbs, indecipherable to the rational mind, indeed probably meaningless. What he intended to convey I imagine was a sort of dark peasant wisdom, something from the deep and mysterious consciousness of the race, the knowledge of centuries gnarled and knotted and knuckled, knobbly and knotted as the hands of an old knaught man. . . . But I am talking like Boddells himself.

He was a round and circular man, stout and voluminously tweeded, patently shrewd, though that may have been a prop, for was not the cunning of the old peasant part of his stock-in-trade? On this particular occasion he responded nobly to Coosins' introduction. Carefully replacing his glass of scotch on the counter, he swung round to face me, paused and stared deep into my eyes for several seconds. Then, equally slowly, he took my hand, wrung it and declared, "You've got to go out, yong man, before you con come in."

Uncomprehending, and thinking that I had perhaps made some frightful social gaffe, I began, I fear, an instinctive move for the door.

Boddells, however, was not done.

"Ye hof te stond before, before ye con look behind."

I glanced over my shoulder, only to be further disquieted by the grave nods with which this particular pronouncement was received by the rest of the company.

Without releasing my hand, Boddells took a gulp of his scotch. Then, raising his voice from the penetrating whisper in which his injunctions had previously been delivered, he suddenly roared at me, "The shortest way round is the longest way home."

There was an audible murmur of applause. Somebody cried, "Ashtowk Paddy, what'll ye have?" Coosins thrust a scotch into my now released hand; everybody beamed. So far from being disgraced, I had been the recipient of wisdom, and for a moment I basked in the glory.

I discovered in the course of the next few minutes that the main danger in this particular segment of the B.B.C. was any attempt to put a rational construction on what was said and to reply accordingly. Best of all was a grave inclination of the head towards the glass in one's hand (or the glass that, all going well, was in one's hand) accompanied every now and then by a keen and penetrating look into the speaker's eyes and a swift laugh whenever it became obvious that the climax of an anecdote had been reached, or that what was said was meant to be funny. Another danger was the attempt to employ genuine

Irishisms in their proper context. These nearly always fell flat, indeed often incurred reproof, whether because they were regarded as unfair, or more likely, as a literary affectation, I cannot say. Of course there was always a fair sprinkling of English about with whom rational conversations could sometimes be held: conversations which had drawbacks, but of a different order.

This occasion however was Celtic to the molars.

To Boddells' left stood another northern Irish versifier, a former businessman called McLoosh. If Boddells represented the dark wells of the racial consciousness, McLoosh was dour, craggy and hard-headed, evoking granite, grey seas and family board-rooms. Coosins on the other hand obviously stood in for the hopeless, impractical, devil-may-care, heart-breaking Irishman of legend, and in spite of a certain glimmer of anxiety occasionally noticeable in his eye he played the part with splendid abandon. There were others, no less Celtic than themselves (and indeed, it might be added, no more) and together their conversation reached extreme and to me somewhat alarming heights of non-meaning.

"It's a wise bird that leaves its own nest," Boddells would declare, amid judicious nods. Or, "As an old mon in the glens said to me once, 'There's many a waiting and wasting and wanting before the lip is cupped and the cup has slipped!'" It must not be thought that he delivered himself of these pronouncements lightly. Though always incomprehensible and sometimes barely audible they were delivered with immense force and conviction. I found them nerve-racking.

Coosins of course was easier to handle, or so in my innocence I thought.

"O bejabers and isn't it yourself that is like a drop of

the cratur when the tongue is lapping the sour milk. We must get you fixed up now before the winter is full upon us and the wind is whistling down Regent Street and Oxford Street and curling into Portland Place itself. O we'll have you fixed up as snug as a snipe in a bog. Whisht up to me now while I tell you. There's room for us all here that can make the words sing and whistle like the birds. Ashtowk Paddy it is not trash you'll be writing for the Home Service or any other service. It is for the third programme that you'll be making the randy words tumble each other like rabbits in the morning sun. Ay," he concluded in a voice genuinely hoarse with emotion, "and if there was a fourth programme aself, it is you that would be on it."

Since such words as I employed in the course of my lugubrious versifications did anything but behave in the fashion indicated I could only receive this in silence, a silence fortunately interrupted by a piercing pronouncement from Boddells.

"The word," he interrupted—he pronounced it "wirred", but too much dialect is wearisome—"the word is like a birred thot's flown."

The company nodded, all but McLoosh, who growled granitically into his glass.

"The wirred"—we might as well—"the wirred hops when it walks ond walks when it hops, but when it flies it falls, and when it falls it feels, but the wirred like the birred flies after its fall, until there is no more falling or feeling at all."

The applause was tumultuous, taking the form of a chorus of "at all, at all's", drowning even McLoosh's granitic growls and creating such a sensation that the cries of "Come up, Mick" and "Puck him, Christy" which other employees of the corporation had been benignly uttering were momentarily stilled.

Under cover of it Coosins jogged my elbow.

"Let you be following after me for a minnit, Paddy, the way a dog would be following after a blind man, down under the ground to the jakes, where it is I would be having a word with you in the privacy of the privy."

Obediently I followed.

In the privacy of the privy Coosins delivered himself of a few more Chinese compliments, then, producing a carefully folded ten bob note, he stuffed it into the top pocket of my jacket.

"Tis I that will have to be going in a few minutes, Paddy, but let you stay on here and be talking to Boddells and McLoosh and the others, as it is only your right to be talking to those that are our own. And bein' one of our own, 'tis you that will be in the pig's belly before a month of Sundays has passed. Take that now to be buyin' a round, for some of those others that are there are very impowrtant people in the jobs line, and I'm sure it's not plenty at you, and 'tis only sorry I am 'tis not more plenty at me, but though I have three verse plays and six repeats before the end of the month, 'tis mortgaged they all are in advance. But next month with the holy help of God, and barring the queen doesn't die on me like her blackguard of a father did last winter causin' me cancellations of four features and eighteen repeats, 'tis three verse plays, a feature and five repeats I'll be havin', and then we'll all be in the pig's belly. And maybe sure 'tis a verse play or two you'll be having yourself by then—ay and even a repeat if the luck was in it."

With visible emotion he wrung my hand. Did I feel the shades of the prison house closing on me once more? Did my notoriously inefficient warning system emit the faintest bleep? Did I, to put it bluntly, sense a trap? I know of course that even at that very moment I must have had misgivings, but let me not magnify it into a moment of crisis. My fall was, after all, a gradual one. It is the essence of this sort of thing that when at last one becomes aware of the situation one is altogether too demoralised to resist.

"Let us be gostherin and goostherin here again tomorrow at the same time till we see what good the ill wind will blow us. I have to run now like a hare, but let you be staying here where the yellow malt is flowing."

He sprinted up the stairs and left me; and thus began what I like sometimes to think back on as my career in the British Broadcasting Corporation. Every day at round about the same time I would leave the Rowton and present myself at the Stork. The last golden leaf-fall, the rose-tinted morning mists of October were already gone. The greasy rains and fogs of November gave way to the frost and sleet of the festal month of December, and these in turn to the first harsh winds of the new year. The posters said "Five Year Old Girl Missing"; then "Shirley: Common Combed". "Shirley: Troops Out", "Shirley: Nation-Wide Hunt" and finally, "Shirley Found Strangled". Some other small victim replaced her in the public consciousness, Christmas came and went, and still I continued regular in my attendance at the pub. I would leave the Rowton in the half-dark of the winter noonday, a last cry of "Ashtowk Paddy!" ringing in my ears, and enter the Stork just as the first merry shouts of "By Jasus I'll ate 'im" and "I'm afther buryin' the mother" inaugurated the lunchtime session. Coosins was often late, but he too was unfailing in his attendance. And every day without fail I received my stipend, the folded ten bob note; sometimes indeed his generosity stretched to a pound. I was, I suppose, in the pig's belly, if not after the fashion originally outlined, at least in a manner of speaking. Out of the ten bob note I dutifully bought my round, swooping down when the pints were three-quarters full or the Scotch drinkers were in need of chasers with a speed acquired on sterner battlefields. Thereafter I reserved two and threepence for the Rowton: the surplus, if any, was mine to spend as I chose: as for eating, you would be surprised at the haste and regularity with which the Corporation's employees ordered plates of sausages which they did not consume.

AS time went by I really began to believe that I too had in fact a job in the Corporation, and so in a way I had. I was certainly as regular in my attendance as most. Because of my somewhat inferior position and lack of skill in the matter of Celticisms I had to suffer a good deal in silence; and as the weeks passed it began to be obscurely apparent even to me that I was being rewarded, as by Prunshios and so many others, largely for my willingness to endure exhortation about the dialoctic and my contribution or lack of contribution to its movements.

It was a somewhat different dialoctic. In the circle in which I moved an unmistakable Celticism of word and spirit was demanded. One was required to subscribe to the tweedy view, at least in theory, as an aesthetic and a way of life: in practice, as I began to see, there were subtle differences between what was permitted and what was not.

Certainly the kind of Celtic *schwarmerei* into which I was rapidly declining was not popular.

Nonetheless the work was not too onerous to be borne, to begin with at least; and though the empyrean heights of Irishry were difficult and dangerous to scale, one could always lose oneself in the background, where an odd cry of " Puck him, Christy ! " was sufficient to get one accepted as a respectable employee of the corporation. Sometimes I was mistaken by aspirant actors for a producer; even a writer had status; and since all the affairs of the corporation appeared to be conducted in the pub, regular attendance there (and God knows mine was regular enough) was in itself a sort of proof of one's credentials. For a while at least I had a sense of belonging and of pulling one's weight in a large organisation, and though I was rather more ill-rewarded than the majority of those I may, even now, be permitted to think of sometimes as my erstwhile colleagues, I had, had I not, the principal satisfaction, that feeling of being happily camouflaged, which is to be obtained from any job?

It must have been during this early, comparatively happy period that Prunshios paid me a visit. Word had begun to spread among my limited acquaintance in the outside world that I had a big job in the B.B.C. and several people had already come to see me in the pub. Beggars from O'Turk's had turned up on at least half a dozen occasions: it had become one of their places of pilgrimage. Most of them departed disgruntled, either because I could not immediately commission several verse-plays with a guarantee of a sufficient number of repeats (verse-plays which I am sure would have been hammered out to any required formula there and then on the counter, for the beggars were nothing if not willing) or because, in spite of my big job, I was peculiarly reluctant to lend them any money. One of them, however, a large ex-farm labourer called Gudgins, had decided to settle there, whether in the status of beggar or fellow employee I was never quite sure; but certainly he also was remarkably regular in his attendance at the pub and I would catch his eye sometimes as he stood in a corner surrounded by the lesser sort of actor and producer, roaring "Ashtowk Paddy!" with the best of them. Though doubtless not in receipt of a regular salary like myself he must have been doing quite well, for on one of the few occasions on which we had any real converse—we were both, I suppose, too busy—he described our place of employment, in apparent gratitude, as "a damn good billet".

The visit from Prunshios, however, was rather a different matter. I am convinced that it represented some sort of climax to my career in the corporation; and it is from that moment perhaps that my downfall began. I was standing one day with a large company which included, as luck would have it, Boddells, McLoosh, Coosins and several celticised anglo-saxons, when the door was thrust open and there, framed against the perpetual London twilight, stood Prunshios; hat, coat, hair and ambience of greatness all complete. I saw him before I heard him, of that I am sure; but in a moment everybody heard him and a hush descended, so that the voice of an Englishman who was muttering "Puck him, Christy" quietly to himself in a corner was suddenly isolated in the silence.

"If my hot," announced Prunshios in awe-inspiring tones, "if my hot blew into a public-house I wouldn't follow it in."

He paused, one hand upraised, while hardened whiskey drinkers disassociated themselves from their glasses.

"But I'll make an excoption. There's a yong mon here thot I wont to see."

Everybody glanced around uneasily, while my heart sank, and with reason.

"I see him here in the company of several Irishmen of note, Billy Boddells, Caspar McLoosh and the bold Walley Coosins himself. A right, good, forward-lookin' yong fellah he is."

Distributing slaps on the back and handshakes at a great rate, his teeth bared to express benign paternalism and common humanity, Prunshios advanced inexorably on my retreating self.

"Well, Caspar, ye hove the right stuff here, what?" he leered at McLoosh, the thinness of whose answering smile was emphasised by the scarcely suppressed granitic fury of his growl.

"Billy, my lad, ye could spot it like me, what? The sharp edge to the front, a mind like a Toledo blade, but not for obstroctions, oh no. This yong fellah is properly wurred in."

He was wringing me by the hand, beaming with indulgent pride on the rest of the company. I could see that even Coosins thought this was going too far and his eye was clouding with anxiety.

Boddells' talent for the non-committal stood him in good stead.

"Ye can be wurred in to your own wirreds, Prunshios," he observed, "ond the wirreds can borrow ond the wirreds can beg, until one wirred borrows another, but there's maybe no more to say."

This may have been simple folk-wisdom, but I could have wished for a different metaphor. Prunshios, however, was used to the patois of the north, and he made not the slightest attempt to elucidate the meaning of the remark. Covering his teeth for a moment to signify the gravity of its import and the depth of his agreement, he then returned to the attack.

"How right ye are, Billy, but I wouldn't doubt ye. Ye know, you yong fellahs here in the B.B.C. are maybe inclined to get a wee bit out of touch. Wirreds are all very fine in their way but the manure is as clean as the seed. There's a danger that ye might get out of touch with the true dialoctic. I'm not saying it's true, mind you, but the danger's there. Ye should live in a slum like this yong fellah here. Ye'll not have yer finger on the pulse of the people at . . ." He was momentarily at a loss . . . "At garden parties and the like of that."

The accusation was intolerably unjust, but Prunshios was visibly proud of his knowledge of the big world. I shuddered for what was to come.

"This yong fellah comes here to London ond the first thing he does is go to live in a doss-house. Thon and thon only he comes to the B.B.C., with his hot in his hond maybe, but with the frosh wunds of the people's vision blowing through his mind. Yer mon enough to see ye hove something new on yer honds, a new whurl of the dialoctic maybe, thot ye can't quite understand, but ye give him the job he deserves because for all yer garden parties and yer cocktail dances yer not entirely out of touch.

"I can feel it already," he cried, "there's a new wund blowing through the corridors of the B.B.C. Ontellectualism is all very well in its way, but ye want to combine yer ontellectualism with the knowledge of the people. Ye want to manure yer ontellectualism. Ye don't want to be afraid of getting down to the level of the working man in the doss-house. Here, let me buy ye all a cocktail."

He motioned imperiously with his hat to the barman. It was a bad moment and I thought I was done for. He was slapping McLoosh on the back and I could hear the cracking of the granite above the wash of the grey seas. I underestimated, however, both the solidity of Ulster and Coosins' never failing resource.

"Oh yer right Prunshios," he cried, "yer right. But there's no wind as fresh as the old wind that blows everybody a bit of good. And if anybody from the ould sod has the dialoctic at his fingertips isn't it you that gave him the good, good grounding in it? But it's not at garden parties that Billy got the words under him, but in the glens themselves, and it is the pure sweet heather of the glens that does be blowing through the corridors of his mind. And if Paddy Riley here would be listening to him it is as much he'd learn as we all know he did from you. Oh, a Toledo blade. Oh, lovely, a Toledo blade. And after that recommendation I wouldn't be surprised if it was the *big* job he would be after getting to do and it is the right school he is studying in with Caspar here who has the words to tear the bejasus out of reality."

Thus distributing compliments impartially and leaving my status as ambiguous as possible Coosins soothed the troubled northerners, so that it was with only the barest edge of minatory asperity in his voice that Boddells began, "There was an old mon in the glens once, Prunshios." And when Prunshios countered with "As an old mountainy woman once said to me, Billy", it was evident that for the moment at least I was forgotten and that the contest was in the nature of a friendly. The lilt of the northern voices as they pursued their interminable anecdotal way was soothing; I began to get over the shock of having my camouflage suddenly ripped from me; the pub got smoothly into gear again—giving, if he had but listened, the lie to Prunshios' libels on the B.B.C.'s inability to reproduce the voice of the people; long before closing time it was ringing as usual with cries of "shplit the bashtard" and "not since the mother".

Nevertheless the damage had been done. From that moment the pressure, I fancied, increased. People began to lecture me about my idleness while they filled the night with words; to sneer at my Irishisms and remark on my clothes. Arising in the all too seasonable morning weather of the early months of the new year, hanging around the Rowton until it was time for the midday session, walking brisk and breakfastless down the Hampstead Road past the furniture stores, the bomb-sites, the caffs, and the vermilion plates of tomato soup on the hoardings, I had ceased to look forward with the old eagerness to my day in the corporation. And I was finding it difficult to effect with any sort of ease or nonchalance the necessary transition between the lunch-time pub and the afternoon club, or the reciprocal movement at half-past five. Other people had the advantage of me here. A ten-minute visit to the office and they would reappear refreshed, rested and glowing with righteousness. I alone had to keep my nose to the grindstone. I would sometimes, right enough, take a walk through the corridors of Broadcasting House, affably saluting such acquaintances as I met on the way; but although these peregrinations were a brief change, I cannot honestly say that they were a real relaxation.

Worse still, the life of pretence that I was leading was leaving me open to the attacks of the most spurious moral imperatives. I actually began to think sometimes that I needed, nay, desired, genuine employment in the organisation. We become what we pretend to be, and I found myself, to my extreme confusion, metamorphosing under my own eyes. The situation was in fact quite simple. As each morning dawned to the clanking and banging of buckets and chamber-pots, the soft swish of urine being poured from one receptacle into another, and the cheerful obscenities of the old women, I had an immediate and pressing need for food and drink and a modicum of ready cash. All these were to be had, after the lapse of an empty three hours or so, in the Stork; and so far as I in my innocence then knew, in the Stork alone. So to the Stork I went.

But as the days in the Stork passed, I began, as often before, to suffer from twisted compulsions and social guilts. I was not avaricious, far from it. I was not anxious for an opportunity to make the randy words tumble each other. Quite the contrary. But I could not have explained this to the company by whom I was surrounded. In the Stork it was expected of me that I should abandon myself with joy to the centripetal suck that would pluck me, if I would but swim a little first, into the very heart of the dervish dance itself. I began to be racked with remorse. But it was not a genuine, pure and unadulterated remorse about failing to get my hands on the cash, or acquiring the prestige of success. Out of sheer social intimidation I began to feel that there was in fact something wrong with me; and if I sprang up in bed among the hawking and spitting third Ypres veterans and the vomiting, urinating and still blasphemous Irish, moaning, as I often did, "synopsis, synopsis", it was not because I bitterly regretted my failure to compose the requested synopsis for the sake of any advantage it might have actually brought me, but simply that it would have set my mind, so far as it was in concert with other peoples' minds, at rest. I could not, I never have been able to experience the pure self-laceration at a wasted opportunity for advancement; no, only the half-hearted but perhaps more wretched guilt that comes from seeing ourselves as others, we imagine, must see us. I desired only peace, but I was foolishly unwilling to be judged lacking in certain normal ambitions. Not for the first time, nor for the last, had I been manoeuvred into allowing my foot to be placed on the first rung of the ladder, so that for all eternity I must be transfixed in that pose: neither saint nor success, but failure. I said to myself, as so often before, that there were only two roads out of this situation, either to go back, which my whole nature yearned for; or to go forward, which I would sometimes attempt by a series of almost invisible convulsions; and of course the result of trying to do both at once was to increase the confusion, aggravate the guilt, and perpetuate the situation which caused them.

It was about this time, shortly after Prunshios' visit, that goaded by somewhat similar moral imperatives and social guilts I got mixed up with the welfare state. As with most of my errors I cannot altogether explain how I came to make it. The Tory newspapers had been full of reports about the vast sums which the welfare state was disbursing to the undeserving poor, and these reports themselves I suppose exercised the same fraudulent moral compulsion on me which my companions in the Stork were generating. Nobody but a fool would refuse to avail himself of the facilities provided in either case.

This, as I must constantly enjoin the reader to remember, is a work of history, and to understand the circumstances requires a certain exercise of the historical imagination. The welfare state was then in full swing. Unemployment had risen sharply throughout the years of Labour administration. You couldn't even get a job shouting "mind the doors" on the underground—this I remember particularly because it seemed to me to be a very creative and satisfying job and represented in a quiet, secretive day-dreamy sort of way, an ideal. I would be down there in the warmth out of the weather all day watching the people come and go, assuaging the histrionic impulse by the delicate shades and nuances that one got into one's roar. There would be a staff canteen and perhaps an opportunity to meet nice girls; in any case I would have my bed-sitter and my gas-ring to go home to. A few years later when the Tory Boom had succeeded the Labour Slump I could have satisfied this ambition quite easily. I might indeed have come to represent an older, sterner, more forthright style of delivery amid the representatives of a fashionable decadence intoning "mind them doors" in the soft accents of the West Indies, been the Martin Harvey or the Quiller Couch of Leicester Square. But in those days it was a day-dream only. There were more men than jobs. The welfare state was in full swing.

One day, however, when my heart was low, I betook myself to a Labour Exchange, a tastefully appointed building in Camden Town, looking like something left over from the Festival of Britain which had been spat on too often and could never be cleanly swept out. There were long queues, appearing to consist of three main classes of persons. There were the gloomy, intent and resentful representatives of the English working classes, the rightful heirs and beneficiaries of the whole set-up. There were the darkies, Maltese,

Cypriots, and Irish, all in fine fettle, exchanging salutations and jokes in a variety of languages and dialects. And there was a third element, nattily dressed, many of them in blazers and silk scarves, occasionally consulting gold watches impatiently when the queue dragged, conversing intently in their own particular argot. Long experience of the Stork and the sight of one or two vaguely familiar faces enabled me to identify these latter as actors. The acrid aroma of what I later recognised as reefers hung heavily in the air. Only the natives argued with the bureaucrats; for their commonwealth cousins and the artists in the blazers the visit appeared to be in the nature of a formality and a not too tiresome social event, something like a publisher's party or the sherry stage of a poetry reading: necessary and useful professionally no doubt, but enjoyable also up to a point.

My turn was long in coming, for I did not know enough to join a queue containing a preponderance of blazers and dark complexions. When at length I reached the counter I was interviewed by a small, long-eared man who appeared even more depressed and miserable than I was. He looked a little like a rabbit and he had a sort of hutch to live in. I did not know then, though I have subsequently learned, that the best thing to do with a petty bureaucrat is to pitch him a plausible tale well within the area of his experience. Tell him something—tell him anything—that will fit his pigeon hole. If you tell him anything else you will not only puzzle and irritate, but frighten him as well. He is like a novelist, who can handle experience provided it is clothed in the required formula: one touch of the truly bizarre or the inexplicable and he is both helpless and worried. For the actors the matter was simple. To their friends they were resting; to the bureaucrat they were temporarily unemployed. He stamped their cards and gave them their money with a smile. The immigrants also were for the most part cut and dried. They had landed on these hospitable shores in full expectation of being allowed to put their hands to the plough. Finding no work available they traversed the hospitable road from the labour exchange to the National Assistance Board. In the first they were solemnly assured that there was in fact nothing at the moment; in the second they collected their money, after which they retired, the Irish to the Rowton and the adjacent pubs, there to continue their temporarily interrupted quarrels; the Cypriots to the room over the caff; the Maltese to check the girls' earnings; the West Indians to the cosy fug of crowded, happy rooms in Notting Hill Gate where the smoke of reefers mingled with the soft sing-song of another clime and the memories of perennial sunshine. The visit to the labour and the formal endorsement of the fact that just at the moment there was nothing for them was a necessary preliminary to drawing the money at the other establishment. One and all they had a moderately happy and humane relationship with the clerks with whom they dealt. Their papers were in order; they were, after all, customers, on whom the clerk depended for his job; they posed no problem whatever. If on occasion they became genuinely desirous of work (to raise the fare home for Christmas perhaps, or, in the case of the Maltese sufficient for a deposit on a two-tone, straight-eight saloon) they climbed down off their high-horse and agreed to register for something that was easier to get, plasterer's mate instead of jig-minder. If times were good they got something; but, as I say, at this particular time, the height and pinnacle of the Labour administration, there was of course nothing doing. This was a great bother to the

English and accounted for the angry looks and indeed words that sometimes passed between them and the clerks; for their Commonwealth cousins it was at worst a minor misfortune, at best a blessing without any sort of a disguise.

All this as I say, I was to learn; at the moment the clerk and I were regarding each other in a mutually suspicious silence.

"Your cards, please."

"I'm afraid I haven't got any."

"What have you been doing?"

"Waiting."

"Everybody's got to wait, that's what they're here for. What have you been doing—you haven't got any cards? Been in the army?'

"Er, no, I mean I've just been sort of hanging about."

"Hanging about? You mean you've been unemployed? Got to have cards for that too you know."

"No, I don't mean exactly I've been unemployed. I just haven't been sort of doing anything, at least since I arrived."

"Since you arrived, eh?" He was getting on to known ground and his eyes which had been clouding cleared a little. "Just got here eh? Where from?"

"Ireland." I decided, rightly, to eliminate my months in the Stork.

"Ireland eh? That's better. Don't sound Irish to me but I suppose you have all sorts. We'll see if we can't fix you up. What've you been doing over there?"

"Well, it's hard to say really, sort of this and that."

"This and that? Well if you can't give it a name I'm sure I can't. You been in trouble or anything? We don't mind. You needn't be afraid of us, and bein' Irish nobody need know, see? Trouble if you was English 'ld be the gap in your cards. But bein' Irish nobody need know, see? You can say you've just arrived."

"Oh no," I assured him, "nothing like that."

"Then what have you been doing?"

"Last?"

"Last."

"Well, actually, the last time I sort of did anything, I was sort of editing a magazine."

"Editing a magazine?" He sniffed at the phrase. "Don't get many magazine editors round here and I'm pretty sure we don't have anything in that line at the moment. Just you hold on a minute."

He disappeared, rabbit-like, into his hutch, a tiny gleam of panic in the corner of one eye. I sensed obscurely that the interview was taking the wrong turning and that it was very necessary to take control of the conversation and direct it towards the subject that really preoccupied me, that of money. He returned with a sheaf of papers in his hand which with agonising slowness he proceeded to leaf through.

"The only thing we seem to have in the clerical line at the moment is the Southwark Borough Council wants an assistant rate-collector. That suit you? For the time being I mean.

"No? Well, it is a bit different I suppose. You should try one of the other exchanges. You see they don't always send things like reporting and that to us. You been a reporter, haven't you?" He looked at me suspiciously, obviously thinking that for some reason or other I had exaggerated my status. "I mean, if you go to one of the other exchanges where they have more clerical—Bond Street's about the best I believe—you'd better say exactly what you've been doing. Not much point in, er, layin' it on. Only makes it harder to get you suited, see?" He smiled at me in what he evidently thought was a disarming fashion, as if pitying my ignorance.

I did not know then that laying it on a bit within the limits imposed by accent and appearance was the real art, that the great masters of welfare stateism were of course highly reluctant to get suited.

"But," I said, "I didn't actually expect you to have a job for me."

"Oh, so you didn't didn't you? Well, what did you expect?"

"The fact is, I haven't got any money."

"Well, look, Mr . . . ?"

"Riley."

"Riley. If you'd been a reporter in England, see, you'd have cards, and you could bring those cards along to us and we'd stamp them and give you your unemployment insurance until such time as you could get yourself suited again, and for a maximum period of six months. But since you haven't been, and since you haven't got any cards, *we* can't give you any money see? We're not allowed by law, and I'm sure with the best will in the world I can't give it to you out of my own pocket, because that in a manner of speaking would be breaking the law, too, see?" He smiled thinly but victoriously at me.

I nodded dumb and contrite assent.

"But what I *can* do . . ." He smiled almost warmly this time. "What I *can* do is to register you for employment, after which you can go to the National Assistance Board, and *if* they're satisfied with your credentials, and *if* they think your circumstances warrant it they *may* decide to let you have some money. After which you can come back here twice a week and sign on and then you can go to the National Assistance Board again, see?"

He smiled quite happily this time, thinking he was out of the wood and that there wasn't going to be anything out of the usual after all.

"Yes," I said, "I see. Though as a matter of fact it's not strictly true that I don't want work. It's just that I didn't expect you to have any. I mean I wouldn't mind taking a job if you had anything that would, er, suit me."

"Oh you wouldn't, wouldn't you? Well, I've already told you we haven't got anything clerical at the moment. Course next week or the week after we might have a bit of book-keeping or something like that."

His eyes were clouding again.

"But that isn't really what I was thinking of. I don't think I'd be any good at all at that sort of thing. What I was thinking of was, if you had a job on the Underground shouting 'mind the doors' or something like that. . . ."

He looked at me reproachfully and reluctantly disappearing again into his hutch. A large darkie at the next window whose affairs had apparently reached some sort of impasse and who had been eavesdropping on our conversation while blissfully sucking his reefer, frowned a conspiratorial warning.

"You don't want to weaken now, man. You got him right where you want him. You stick by that editor jazz and he'll be out on pension before you done drawin' your money."

My interlocutor returned.

"Nothing on London Transport," he announced briskly. "You can go and ask them if you want to, but we'd know see? Now, Mr. Riley, the best thing we can do is to get you registered. Then we'll have everything in order and we can proceed from there. Seems to me you've got some funny notions what this is all about. You come in here and say you've been a reporter. . . . Then you tell me it's general clerical and now you want a job as a station attendant. I can put you down as unskilled if you like, but I can't see you carrying a hod, an educated man like you. It wouldn't be right. Now what's it to be? Clerical or reporter?"

"Have you got anything for a driver?" I asked, shyly naming another unfulfilled ambition.

"No drivers," he said briskly. "We've got hundreds of them on the books. Clerical or reporter? Course, we *could* always say you were self-employed in Ireland and then you could take your pick of what was going. Would that be true, in a manner of speaking? Mind you, some of the things we have to send self-employeds to don't really suit."

"Editor," I said, the darkie's eyes upon me.

FROM the labour I progressed to the National Assistance Board. It was Festival of Britain too, but more so, as befitted a place where the Welfare State actually gave away money. Yet, unlike the labour it was subtly infected with a malaise belied by its decorations. It was as if the chamberpot smell from the Rowton hung an inch or two from one's nostrils, not quite inhalable, but there. Perhaps it was, too, the mixing of the sexes that gave rise to a feeling of unease. The cheerful concerns of the West Indians were shadowed by the presence of so many anxious, middle-aged women, peculiarly shifty-eyed compared to the bland criminals from the labour.

After some delay I got talking to a man in a hutch. Editor, yes. Just arrived from Ireland. Ah. Address, Rowton House, Camden Town.

"Seems an odd place for a man of your education?"

This emphasis on learning, which, incidentally I do not possess, seemed to me both irrelevant and excessive.

"Where do you suggest I should go?" I asked.

"Things are not too good in the editing line at the moment, Mr. Riley? Well, we all have our bad times, our ups and downs, our ins and outs. And what can we do for you?"

I explained my dilemma. No job, no money. I adverted to the fact that the Welfare State existed to provide for such contingencies.

"I understand that you are destitute, Mr. Riley?"

"Yes."

"No savings account, no bank account, no wife in regular employment. Parents or other close relatives not residing at the same address and contributing to maintenance. H'mm. How long are you paid up at Rowton House for?"

"Paid up?"

"Yes, haven't you got a ticket?"

"Well, I've got last night's ticket somewhere."

"Ah." He beamed happily at me. "Then from our point of view you are not of course currently resident at Rowton House at all. At the moment, Mr. Riley, from our point of view, from our official point of view, you are destitute and of no fixed address. Well, Mr. Riley, I am empowered to give you an authorisation to the warden of a Salvation Army hostel, or other relief centre, entitling you to a bed in the dormitory for one week and one week's meals in the centre. We will further provide you with the sum of five shillings per week for, er, incidental expenses."

This was a bit of a facer. I had not the slightest doubt that my commonwealth cousins did better than this for themselves. Still, there was a tiny, miserable bit of compensation for my wasted day concealed in it.

"Can I have the five shillings now?" I asked.

"Oh no, Mr. Riley. As a man of some intelligence you will appreciate that we cannot hand out money to people who walk in here off the street and admit that they are resident nowhere." He smiled thinly. "That would be a bit too Irish, wouldn't it? Any casual passer-by as you might say could just pop in here and get some cash."

At a near-by hutch a West Indian in a dazzling shirt and wide-brimmed hat was collecting five pounds and some silver. As I had entered the building two Irishmen had passed me, jovial and beaming, still counting.

"No, Mr. Riley, you would have to go and present your authorisation to the warden of the appointed centre, have it stamped and then return here."

This was not at all what I had expected. The rumour, widely current in the Tory press, of the Welfare State's munificence had evidently been much exaggerated. Yet I could see with my own eyes that some people were contriving to extract hard cash from it.

"I think I'll stay on in the Rowton," I said.

"Just as you please, Mr. Riley. But from our point of view you must remember that you are not actually resident in a Rowton House at the moment and we have no authority to maintain you in one, any more than in the Ritz Hotel."

It was all very puzzling but I was too dispirited to pursue the matter further. I had about ninepence ha'penny, and I turned into a pub across the way to get the taste of bureaucracy out of my mouth. A small old man, wrinkled, capped and mufflered, rather like one of my pensioners, but somewhat dirtier and more dishevelled, was standing next to me at the counter.

"Wot's the maher, mite? Nnt ye geh anyfing?" He asked, as I stared sombrely at my glass. "Proper loh o baasterds they are in they? Ai can tell yeh, Aint easy te geh anyfing aht eh that shaaer."

"You're telling me," I said.

"Ai em telling you," he said. "No mistike. Yeh know where ai'm livin' mite? At the Sally. That's right, Salvyshin perishin' army. Pryers 'n bread 'n margarine fer brefes, dinner 'n tea. Thirty-faive ev es in the sime dawrmitory, 'n a pri-hy filthy loh some eve em awre too, ai c'n tell yeh. Thah's no life mite, noh for a man that's used te the Raahten i' isn't. Ye know sompfen? Ef ai c'ld raihse the praice of a ticket in the Raahten that shaaer 'd have teh keep me there fer the rest eh mai laife."

"You mean that?" I said.

"That's raight mite. One ticket te the Rahten 'n thet's my residence. Have te keep me there, *with* vouchers fer the cahnteen *'n* ther miserable faive bob a week Billy Bunter bloody pocket money."

"But," I said, "a ticket to the Rowton's only two and threepence. What's more, I've got one, but they wouldn't keep me. Offered to send me to the Sally too."

"Nah, nah mite, thet's a dily ticket, thet's no good. Ye get thet in the evening 'n it's aht o dite when ye get up in the mawrnin, so it's not worth a light when ye get te the N.A.B. Wot ye want's a weekly ticket. Fifteen 'n nainepence. Then yer a resident when ye go in there see, 'n they cawn't do nothin' abaht it. Got te keep ye there fer the rest oh yer natural if necessary—least until yeh start gettin' the old age pension, then o' course they tikes it aht o' thet."

"By Jesus," I said. "But there's no way of getting up in the world except by your own initiative. I mean you're stuck in the Sally till you can raise a nicker, in or about."

"You're raight there maite. Seems odd, do-hen't? Course when I was workin', two years ago come April, ai was in lodgins; then wen ai was gettin me unemployment benhefit ai moves into the Rahten teh saive money; 'ad a few bets on the gee-gees one week; goh into deh te mai maites an 'ad teh go to the Sally. Waile ai'm in the the Sally me benhefi' gives aht. 'ff ai'd a spen me las' weeks benhefi' movin' back into the Rahten ai'd a been awreight; but ai gets ih on a Friday, 'as a few bets on the Sa-hurdaiy, an' there ai am ever since Gawd straike me; 'n wats more maite there ai'll be baiy the looks o' it, cawse ai' 'aven't goh the strength te work no longer, even if there was any work 'n they was to offer me any at the labour. Dahn 'n aht maite, thet's wor ai am, me thet wos respec-hebal all me laife, 'n dahn 'n aht ai'll staiy ef ai cawn't raise a nicker prehy soon."

"Well, well," I said. "It seems to me that the motto of the Welfare State is 'to him that hath shall be given'. But tell me, I hear stories of blokes getting five or six quid a week out of them, chaps just off the boat and what not."

"Oh well, o' course that's simple maite. Just as they'd 'ave to keep me in the Rahten if ai was in the Rahten, so they'd 'ave to keep me in a room 'ff ai wos in a room, 'n no fuckin' vouchers fer no canteen, but 'ard cash 'n feed yerself, or 'ave a paint, or go te the dogs, or Bob's yer flippin uncle. These chaps don't 'ave rooms, no more than you 'n me, sleepin on the floor most like, six or seven of 'em at a taime, but they goh pals wot says they 'as rooms, says they let's 'em a room or a shaire in a room fer two or three quid a week, no law against thet, no way o' provin' it, they stick's together maite, 'n wen the bloke comes rahnd from the N.A.B. they says, course he lives 'ere, pays three quid a week for the privilege, 'n the N.A.B. they goh te give it to 'im see, 'n another couple o' quid te feed hisself. Course some o' 'em when they gets the first week's money, they goes off 'n gehs a room, 'n then they gehs a job cause they goh a start in laife, see? They're noh dahn 'n ahts laike me. Their pals stan's in wi' 'em, 'n then the N.A.B. they goh te cawf up, see?"

He looked at me speculatively.

"You a Paddy, maite?"

I nodded.

"You should be aible te work that dodge easy enuff. Aint ye goh 'ny pals woh come over 'ere 'efore ye 'n goh fixed up laike drawin' ther money, thet cld saiy they wos lettin' you a room for three or four quid a week?"

I thought of Coosins and Bodgers and McLoosh.

"I'll have a look round," I said. "I'll think it over."

"Maike no mistaike, maite," he said. "Once that N.A.B. gehs the drop on you they never lets up. Buh you geh on your feet for faive minutes, 'n they 'as te keep you there, see?"

I FOUND my contact with the Welfare State ineffably and curiously depressing. I am easily discouraged but it had something about it which was deeply antipathetic to my nature. The Tory papers were quite wrong. Far more than private Victorian charity it favoured only the deserving poor. And here let me expound the Law of the First Step,

Riley's Law, product of bitter experience, of the first step: If the first step has not been taken, and taken correctly, you might as well be idle as trying to take the second. Let me put it this way. Most people accept as an axiom that money makes money, but it is generally forgotten that without money no money can be made. In other words if a man is absolutely destitute, he cannot rise except through the irrational operations of fortune, and there is no use telling him to make an effort, be a good boy, pull his socks up etc. But, you may say, what about thievery, or beggary, surely these are within the power of everybody who is not absolutely bone lazy, no good inside or out? The answer, I fear, is no. In my experience for thievery or beggary to be carried to a successful outcome a certain minimum of equipment is necessary, without which no one stands a chance. A man who has not eaten for three days, who has no bus fare, whose appearance is so bedraggled that he is liable to be removed to a de-lousing centre by the first policeman he meets, cannot really put up much of a show as a thief or as a beggar, except maybe for an odd penny in an alleyway. To get anything you have to have something: a suit of clothes, the price of a first drink in the pub, an ingratiating manner, sufficient food or drink or money to give you confidence to acquire more, what poor Scott called mobility and grace, a penknife perhaps, or even, God help us, a pen and paper, leisure to mature one's schemes, or one's rubbish for the B.B.C., a bed to have slept in, shoes to walk in, in the case of rich women a preliminary flash of the taxi-fare at least, not to speak of such other matters as a shave, a shirt, the aforementioned suit and what-not. My man in the pub, who could never get out of the Sally, was a living exemplar of Riley's Law, the Law of the First Step. Sink below the first step and you are undone, permanently and terribly undone, except as I say for the irrational operations of fortune, and as far as they are concerned one must remember that they are vastly more likely to favour a man who is active, talkative, acquainted with many who may be the agents of fortune, and of course, let's face it, able to drag himself from one place to another in order to avail of the rumoured opportunity, or, come to that, to insert pennies in the phonebox. Precious little use, in my opinion at least, talking about the irrational operations of fortune to a man who is lying naked, on a pile of rags, in some unfrequented hole or untraversed corner, unable to stir hand or feet because of the need to conserve his last remaining energies, or the fear of bringing on diarrhoea, or some variety of the jigs.

I think it is true to say that around this time I sank below the first step. I had never had much love for the Stork nor inclination to pursue my career in the B.B.C.; whatever enthusiasm (there should be a thesaurus of weaker words) I had ever been able to muster had now completely ebbed away. The Welfare State was obviously not going to be any help to me. It was designed for the respectable proletariat, who would never fall below that fatal first step, and though thieves and chancers from Ireland and the West Indies could avail themselves of it, that was because they stepped ashore on the first step. They had organisation and backing, which I had not. They were orthodox, that is to say, respectable.

There was one last episode which I think of as connected with my career in the corporation, as part of it, though in strict truth of course it was not, just as, in even stricter truth, of course I had no career in the corporation at all. Coosins' bounty aside, it was beginning to be plain that something would have to be done. It was possible to live, and to live moderately well, on the stipend he allowed me, though the work was arduous; but it allowed no possibility of replacing articles of clothing or other necessaries, and I was beginning to be looked upon with disfavour in the Stork. They were all pretty natty dressers there, and tweeds were almost essential if one went in for the Irish act. The miscellaneous collection of oddments that I had acquired as time went by and it became necessary to replace one article or another was not at all the thing. I believe that the showerproof coat, of a particularly obnoxious fawn colour, which I had acquired one day in a public lavatory where I was shaving, was looked upon with great disfavour. I wore it partly because it was winter-time, but principally to cover what was underneath: at least I spared them that, Boddells and McLoosh and the rest of them. It was as I say of a particularly evil colour; it was anything but clean; and it was far too short, so that I looked like a rapidly growing schoolboy in it; furthermore I had to wear it all the time, even when, at three o'clock, the company removed from the pub to the club; and I believe it to have been a most unpopular garment.

Certainly my general popularity in the corporation seemed to be on the decline. I was no longer wafted into any company I cared to join. McLoosh had given up addressing me altogether; and Boddells only did so because it gratified him to impart gnomic wisdom and advice to me, to bully me with proverbs and beat me with examples, all in stern contrast to my situation, all celebrating energy, and resource and what-not, allegedly Celtic virtues far from my grasp and further from my sympathies. In fact I think it is true to say that my position was fast worsening; even Coosins wore a more than usually distracted air when he talked to me; and the ten bob note was now passed to me by a process that resembled telegraphy. The day, I could see, or almost see, was approaching when I would have to leave the security of the corporation for the hurly burly of the outside world.

In fact what transpired was that I acquired, for the first and last time in my life, a patron. Since this relationship is a matter of some importance, it is perhaps worth giving a pretty full account of what it was like and how it came about, so that my experiences may be a guide and to some extent perhaps a warning to others. I was standing one day in the Stork, in my broken shoes and my short fawn raincoat, nursing a half of bitter I had been forced to buy for myself, when Coosins appeared, wearing a more than usually distracted air, telegraphed the ten bob note into my pocket and left the pub instantly.

Within a matter of minutes, however, he was back, and apparently open to offers. I bought him a drink. I was past caring.

"You're looking a bit under the weather, Paddy," said he, eyeing me critically. "You don't look as if you were exactly on the top of your form."

In the Stork among the Celts this was a terrible allegation, so I hurriedly threw out a Celtic witticism or two. They appeared to satisfy him.

"I wonder, Paddy," he said, "if you could possibly oblige till the day after tomorrow with the loan of a half of a crown?"

As I have averred, I was past caring, so I fished a half of a crown out of the garments I wore under the raincoat and passed it to him.

"I'll tell you Paddy," he said, "why I want it. I'm engaged to dine with a lady in Hampstead this blessed evening, and to tell you the truth I had no means of getting there, either by transport public or private." He paused, evidently debating something within himself. "I wonder if you'd fancy a plate of hot scoff yourself? " he asked. "To tell you the truth, Paddy, though I dine with this lady fairly frequently, there are occasions when it is likely to be a bit of a strain unless there is other company present, and I have an uneasy sort of a class of a feeling that this may be one of them. By a curious freak of chance I have a sportscoat and a sort of a class of a pair of flannels in a suitcase here in the pub. I took them off in a shop some years ago when my situation improved and I was in the way of purchasing tweeds, and they've been in cold and hot storage here ever since. We could outfit you now, purely on a loan basis of course, and not casting any aspersions on your appearance as it stands."

Against the protests of the barman the antediluvian suitcase was fetched out and I donned the garments in the lavatory. The sportscoat wasn't a bad fit, but the flannels were of an order which had long since disappeared from the golf-links and seafronts of the world. They had the native tendency of that kind of flannel to bag, and since my friend was longer than I they hung about the lower part of my legs in folds, beginning where the short fawn raincoat left off and having a sort of accordion-like, collapsible appearance. If I dwell on these garments now, it is because the reader must imagine me as permanently outfitted in them from here on. The collapsible trousers surmounted by the short fawn dustcoat became my trademarks, what they nowadays call a brand image.

It was snowing as we proceeded to the tube at Oxford Circus and snowing as we emerged from it at the other end. As we trudged with our heads down into the wind, Coosins gave me some advice.

"Whip that old coat off, Paddy, as soon as I ring the bell."

"But it's snowing," I protested. "I'll catch my death of cold if I get wet. My shoes are leaking and my socks are ringing wet already."

"Matter a damn, Paddy. First impressions are everything. You'll make a much better first impression if you whip off that mackintosh or whatever it is before you get into the hall."

We sloshed on, I with my soles flapping. Then we came to a pub.

"I'll tell you what, Paddy," said Coosins. "If you could advance me another two bob for two weenchy little halves of bitter in the hope that they will add to our air of expectancy and joy as we arrive, I'll take care to let you have the whole lot back as soon as I have a private word with Amelia."

Recklessly, I parted. In the pub he told me something of the charms of the lady we were going to see. There was a perceptible shiftiness in his discourse, as if he were justifying himself in advance because of some opinion or other I might form as to his motives and general character.

"Mind you, Paddy," he said. "It might be hard to tell what age she is. She's seen a good many summers come and go. But a beautiful body still, a bee-utiful body. The face shows her age a bit all right, whatever the hell age she is. But not the body. The body is bee-utiful still. And she's had a lot of experience, she's a priestess of the mysteries. Though I grant you that you might not think it to look at her, she's wonderful in bed, woonderful, a priestess of the mysteries of love."

I listened to these revelations in a silence through which I tried to project a modulated but perceptible disapproval.

"Is the lady wealthy?" I enquired.

"Waylthy, is it?" cried Coosins. "She has a cotton plantation out in Sierra Leone, Paddy, as big as Wales. A cotton plantation. As . . . big . . . as . . . Wales. Mind you," he added, the glow fading a little from his eyes, "she's a bit near. You know what the English are like in these matters. A bit punctilious about the money side of it. Not like our poor wandering selves. But that's maybe because she has an orderly mind, a precision instrument, a beeutifully disciplined intellect, like a great and intricate civilisation, cultured and imaginative, but orderly. A powerful mind, Paddy, but it doesn't crush the flowers. That verse programme of mine about the little fairies that was repeated twice last week, the freshness of her mind, Paddy, lay on that like the sweet dew on the grass itself. Of course to tell you the truth, like many powerful intellects she's a weenchy, weenchy little bit opinionated. Such is the strength of her lovely mind, Paddy, that I find her just maybe a little inchy, binchy bit overpowering. My own poor wandering wits seem to shrink a bit, you know?"

I sympathised. I did know.

"She wants to have me psycho-analysed," continued Coosins quite glumly. "Of course she knows all about that sort of thing. She's as contemporary as a new potato and she knows the various theories backwards—she has two or three different kinds of practitioner herself—working away on her bedad, like steam-hammers. It's not that I don't respect her opinion on these matters, for I do. It's just that I don't fancy the idea somehow. It seems to me it would be a waste of everybody's time."

I sympathised again. Psycho-analysing Coosins would be rather like trying to dig a hole in the sea.

"In short, Paddy," he concluded, somewhat surprisingly, "she is one of those wonderful women whose rich Autumn, whose Indian summer of the body and of the mind, has a fascination, an attractiveness, a mysterious bee-uty that outshines the freshness of other women's mornings."

With that we downed our halves of bitter and sloshed on through the snow towards the paragon's house. It stood in its own not inconsiderable gardens a little way back from the road. It was clear that the cotton plantation was thriving, backs bent under the lash in the cruel heat of the Sierra Leonian sun.

"Whip off that old coat now, Paddy," said Coosins in an undertone as he reached out for the bell. Reluctantly I divested myself of the detested garment and stood perishing in the bitter cold. I had been a little surprised at the comparative lack of Celticisms in my companion's conversation so far, and had put it down to a preoccupation, indeed a foreboding, perhaps a guilt that he seemed to feel about the approaching encounter. But in this respect Coosins was nothing if not game.

The door was opened by the lady herself: attired, presumably because she had been cooking the supper with her own fair hands, in an apron, and indeed looking in general not unlike a sharpish, elderly cook-general in a settled and prosperous household.

"Come you out, Amelia," cried Coosin roguishly as she blinked at us from the doorway. "Come you out into the mysterious night and let the snow be after kissing your bee-utiful hair. And let me be after kissing the snow that is kissing it. And I want you to meet Paddy Riley while we stand in the mysterious night, for that is how a poet should come to a house, out of the night and the snow and the mysterious darkness."

Amelia, who at first go-off had seemed inclined to receive us rather coldly, now obediently simpered forward into the slush, and the snow-kissing ceremony was performed while I stood murderously by in my nether garments and broken shoes.

"This, Amelia," said Coosins at length, "is a poet and a true poet from the island of poets in the west, a poet of the grand company of Caspar and Billy, and I have brought him to you out of the night."

"And what a beautiful night it is," said Amelia, taking my corpse-like hand. "Don't you feel that a mysterious change comes over the world when it snows? One of Jung's disciples says that snow is not a symbol of purity but of orgiastic oblivion."

"I'm afraid I'm not in any humour for enjoying it," I said. "My shoes are unfortunately leaking."

"Oh how mundane, how mundane," said the lady, "for a poet and an Irish poet. How literal you are." She laughed lightly and led the way into a richly carpeted hallway full of carefully lit pieces of abstract sculpture. "Wipe your shoes on the scraper, both of you, before you come in," she said. "I don't want my carpet ruined."

We ate in the kitchen. We had rice and fried bananas and fried eggs, the whole being given some Spanish name that I disremember, though in my opinion the Spanish people, who are big eaters, would have rejected it indignantly except as a preliminary to six more courses. I reflected gloomily that I would have done every bit as well off the remains of the sausages in the Stork, and probably better as far as drink was concerned, for all that was produced was one bottle of Algerian rough redders. If the cost of the equipment in a kitchen may normally be considered as the equivalent of one thousand meals, the cost of the equipment, the self-perpetuating electric stove, with alarm clocks, loudspeakers and infra-red devices attached, in this particular kitchen, was the equivalent of at least one million such meals as we ate.

Nor was I allowed to enjoy it, such as it was, in peace. Quickly, expertly, Amelia probed my wounds, or alleged wounds. She established the fact that I lived in a doss-house; that I had no job, or other orthodox source of income, cotton plantations or the like of that; that I accepted shamelessly such charity as came my way; that as far as sex was concerned I was most unlikely, given my circumstances, to enjoy frequent or orthodox satisfactions; and that I appeared to lack any thorough-going ambition to change these circumstances.

It did not seem to occur to her that conversely I did not complain about them. She did that. In spite of Coosins' elephantine efforts to divert the conversation down Celtic byways, I was given, in swift succession, short courses on psychology, respectability, money and poetry, Freudian sexology, Jungian sexology, the poetic benefits of having a job—with some reference to Caspar McLoosh, Billy Boddells and other popular versifiers of the day—the wardrobe of the man of letters—with some reference to the clientele of the Stork—the necessity to shave every day, the necessity to procure for oneself a modest furnished room in a cheap part of London and from therein to bombard the B.B.C. with synposes, the absolute necessity to procure and maintain a job in order to obtain and sustain such an apartment.

My ability to concentrate on all this was lessened by a stink that began to arise in the course of it from under the table at which we sat. It was the effect of the soaking followed by the drying on my socks, which were invested by the fungus growth which is the cause of the condition known as tinea pedis or athlete's foot. The fungus, loosened and liquified by the soaking, was now polluting in the heat. Amelia fortunately did not notice the noxious smell which was the result, for she was at the other end of the table, but Coosins, who was at right angles to me, did, and it naturally increased his mental discomfort greatly. This had already been, in my judgment, acute; and I noticed too that though he adequately fulfilled the minimum conditions laid down for me, he did not escape occasional sharp censure. However often repeated Coosins was, Amelia had the upper hand morally. It went with the plantation.

At length Coosins seemed unable to bear the moral tone of the conversation any longer, to say nothing, probably, of the stink. Rising from the table he spread out his arms and suggested "a dander through the wild night to the tavern in the snow, where the darts will be darting in the firelight". Naturally, I was enthusiastic, and Amelia, though dubious morally, was persuaded by further Celticisms to venture. We sloshed out into the wild night.

Things got off to a bad start. Coosins was unable to buy the first drink and Amelia would not. I plonked down my last three bob. Unless Coosins did his stuff I would be homeless in the snow. Coosins suggested a game of darts, presumably to avoid further conversation with Amelia's great intellect. She had to don glasses in order to be able to see the board and this seemed to render her easier to handle. Coosins began to gain ground. He jollied her into two or three rounds. I began to have hopes of my ten bob. We were almost enjoying ourselves.

When she went to the counter again he followed her,

presumably to request a little ready cash, but I could see at once that the going was sticky. He seemed to pass from Celtic drollery, to Celtic raillery, to desperation; but as far as I, waiting at the dartboard, could see, there was no cash transaction. I was grateful to him for his efforts of course; and I realised that the original ten bob note had been his; but it was still true that my simple regimen had been disturbed and a sequence on which I had been led to rely interrupted for no reason except that I might suffer an evening of even more than usual moral discomfort and, probably, so that Coosins would have a companion through whose conversation he might escape some of the moral animus usually directed towards him on such domestic evenings. The net result of the whole thing, as far as I could see at the moment, was that I would be left to wander in my broken shoes through the snow until such time as my corpse was discovered and taken to the mortuary to thaw. I wondered where Coosins lived. The atmosphere of domesticity was strong and I suspected he lived in the house. It had been obvious from several of the none too obliging or civil references made to him that he was a familiar inmate. I made up my mind to request sanctuary for the night. The house was large enough in all conscience. Phrases about dogs and orphans burgeoned inchoately in my mind as I imagined the night beyond the pub and tried to work up some anger. Failing shelter I thought I would ask for five bob, which would get me to the Rowton, in, and back to the Stork.

They returned from the counter, Coosins waggling his head and winking behind her, evidently attempting to convey some reassurance or warning to me. There were about twenty minutes to go and for those twenty minutes he kept up a constant flood of Celticisms, a performance which could not but be admired, however distantly. Demoralised by uncertainty, and by the necessity for action and utterance, I could not be of any help. It was one of those cases, alas so common, where one's prospect of charming one's way to success is diminished by the anxiety which the prospect of asking creates.

I decided to plead for shelter first and for money only as a last resort. The conditions of the night were such that any man not possessed of a snow-plough might reasonably ask for a doss-down without incurring another moral lecture about his poverty and weakness. If I could have had a word with Coosins in the jakes I would gladly have consulted him about what was best to be done, but I could get no opportunity either to signal or speak to him in private, and, though I wasted precious time by going twice myself in the hope that he would follow, he failed to do so.

With five minutes to go I took the plunge. "Amelia," I said lightly and pleasantly, "do you think it would be possible for you to put me up? The night is so bad and I have such a long way to go."

She laughed, lightly and pleasantly. "Oh Paddy," she said, "you're incorrigible. What a thing to ask after all we've just said this evening. And I thought we'd agreed to embark on a course of rehabilitation." Her expression became serious and concerned. "No, Paddy," she said. "I would gladly put you up but I don't think it would be good for you psychologically. I think what you need to practise now is absolute self-reliance. I would say a great deal of this dependence of yours on other people is simply an attempt to prove yourself so loved that everybody is prepared to look after you. It's a by no means uncommon syndrome and I think we must try and arrange for you to be treated—at a public clinic of course. But in the meantime I don't think your friends should encourage you in these practices in any way."

"H'mm," I said. "Fair enough. Though to tell you the truth I don't think there's anything wrong with me that a shower of fivers wouldn't cure. Still, if your religion forbids you to put me up for the night, do you think you could lend me five bob?"

She laughed again, this time quite heartily.

"Oh Paddy, Paddy," she cried. "Don't you see that that proves everything I have been saying? First of all you ask me to put you up for the night because it is snowing and you have a long way to go. Then having failed in that, and, incidentally, proved the motive behind it to be false you immediately try something else, quite different, because you unconsciously wish to prove that you are entitled to depend on other people for anything you want and that you can successfully do so."

I was about to try to explain to her about the Rowton, but I could see Coosins performing a sort of fire-dance behind her back, hopping ponderously up and down from one foot to the other, jigging and grimacing, his face a contorted mask of agony. He was gesturing towards himself spastically with his thumb. Unfortunately I misunderstood him.

"Perhaps Wally could put me up," I ventured. "Could you Wally?"

Amelia's expression, which before had been good-humouredly reproving, changed suddenly for the worse.

"Where?" she cried, addressing Coosins. "Where are you talking about?" addressing me.

Sensing that I had put a brick in it, I was about to try to say something in reply when Coosins broke in. "Ah Paddy, don't you know that if I had rooms, or palaces either, yes or a tinker's shelter under a ditch indeed, or a pig-sty itself, 'tis you would be as welcome to them as the first cuckoo that comes across the bitter sea. But 'tis in Amelia's that my head is resting at the moment, and though it would be a great draught for the heart to have you there as well, 'tis Amelia that knows all about the depth psychology and the like of that, so though it goes against my poor simple grain to agree with her, I think you should be after trusting her bee-utiful mind and believing that it will be the best for you and for the psychology in the latter end if you make your way to your lodgings tonight."

I thought it was unlike Coosins, who after all was generous and big-hearted to a degree, to abandon one to freeze so lightly. Yet he was being absolutely no help. Did he not know how desperate my situation was? He seemed frightened of something and Amelia continued to gaze at him short-sightedly and suspiciously.

Then the dog-like barmen gathered barking round us, and in a mutually hostile and bewildered silence we were shepherded to the door.

I slowed my pace to a mere paralytic crawl, so that Amelia should go first and I might have a word with Coosins. But it was absolutely no use. She took his arm like a sixteen year old and jerked him outward into the night. Then, gaily, she turned to me, waving and smiling under a street-light in the falling snow.

"Good night, Paddy," she trilled. "Do come again sometime. I'm fascinated by your case, you incorrigible old thing."

They started across the road, Coosins apparently afflicted with some sort of Saint Vitus's dance, his head bobbing up and down towards me, the right side of his face altogether disassociated from the left. Half way across she turned. "Be sure and ring up first, Paddy," she crooned. "I'm sometimes very busy with Wally's scripts."

Then they were gone and I was alone in the falling snow, my socks soaking in the moisture. I recollected that my abominable dustcoat was clutched under my arm. I put it on and experienced some slight sense of relief. It was a shelter, of a kind. For a second or two I was almost cosy.

Then the full extent of my situation struck me. Where was I to go? What was I to do? I had been homeless before, but rarely with warm interiors so near at hand and so utterly shut against me, and never in the snow. I started up the hill cursing, principally to keep myself warm. I have found from long experience that when you are homeless at night, it is essential to have an objective. I have often reached a pitch of ecstasy while on the march towards a definite objective, thinking my old thoughts and dreaming my old dreams, that many a man snug at home in his bed might envy. Of course you get a bit of a turn when you draw a blank, but I have often spent a preponderantly ecstatic night marching from one objective to another, drawing a blank here or a blank there, but regaining the old ecstasy as I set out again. The worst periods in such a night are the indecisions as to whether to ring or not, having arrived, with the lights out; the foostering up and down little-known roads trying to identify the house correctly; the attempts to gain entrance to interior apartments while by-passing hostile and communal front-doors. I am not at all sure whether, on many such a night, I might not have been happier on a long march towards a distant and putative objective not to be reached until breakfast time, but, because of a miscalculation about distance, regarded as a distinct possibility nonetheless. It all goes to show something about the fruition of desire. But back to my story.

I marched on towards the tube, though I had nothing to do with tubes, because it represented a lighted, sheltered, partially warmed spot where I might pause to meditate; because there is always the faint hope that you may meet somebody sympathetic either entering or leaving one of these places; because it was more likely that an idea might come to me there than in the falling snow; and, perhaps most important of all, because it represented a limited, practical objective, with some slight vestige of hope attaching to it, on the march towards which I could recover from the shock and suspend all further deliberations about the next step.

I was getting almost into good spirits, sloshing uphill in the snow, when I heard a noise behind me, a sort of wet pounding and breathing, as if I was being pursued by a polar bear or worse. I stopped and turned. It was Coosins. He came abreast of me.

"Ah Paddy, and is it yourself heading into the cold darkness of Hampstead? I couldn't say a word there, partly out of respect for Amelia's bee-utiful mind, and partly because there are things that with all her great and bee-utiful understanding of psychology she'd maybe better not know. I tried to signal you to wait a wee while outside the pub till I escaped myself for a minnit on the plea of walking in the garden in the snow and thinking of the orgasm. I have here the key of a house and chiming beside it is the key of a wee room where you may sleep this night, ay and many another night too. I have to fly now, but let you be going on to Sissons Road where the number that you will find written on the door is number thirty-seven and the room is on the left on the first landing."

I slept that night of snow away in Coosins' room, a small apartment of the usual furnished variety with a gas fire and ring, a single chair and a bed. Rarely did I pass a snugger night. My escape had been miraculous and I listened to the wind in ecstasy. Going over it all in my mind, I could only suppose that anxiety of a different kind had prevented him from being more forthright or arousing Amelia's suspicions by following me to the jakes. Next day, just when I was about to set out for the Stork, he appeared. He was genuinely contrite but he thought I had understood that I was to wait a minute or two outside the pub while he collected the key and made his escape.

Amelia did not know that he had a room elsewhere, which he maintained, I now gathered, for the entertainment of one or two other beautiful bodies of his acquaintance. She must at all costs not know. She had taken a great fancy to my case and would be delighted to see me again. I was bidden to supper three nights later. Meanwhile I was more than welcome to the room, provided we could arrange a series of signals and means of communication which would indicate when he was actually entertaining company and inform me when he wished to. Since we met in the Stork every day; there was a telephone on the landing outside; and arrangements of blinds and window curtains were not beyond our joint devising, this was a practicable proposition. We left for the Stork together, I congratulating myself on a good step up in the world. Little I knew.

The supper three nights later was one of the low points of my entire career. There were present, besides Amelia, her undergraduate daughter, Coosins and myself, none other than Boddells, McLoosh and one or two other familiar faces from the Stork. I should have thought that such a distinguished company would have something better to occupy them than my poor failings, but no. Expertly and rapidly, Amelia manoeuvred the conversation round to psychiatry and from there it was but a short step to me.

"I find Paddy's case fascinating," she said. "You all probably know more about it than I do, since I believe he spends most of his time cadging and begging from you in the Stork. It is very interesting that a person of Paddy's intelligence and talents should allow himself to sink into a position of absolute dependence on other people, should actually enjoy being a sponge."

"Very," murmured the daughter, a not undesirable girl of twenty, who was studying sociology and was of course heiress to the cotton plantation. "Were you breast-fed when you were a baby?"

Amelia and I both ignored the interruption. "I was talking about Paddy to my psychiatrist," continued our hostess. "She was fascinated by what I told her and I must say she approved of my diagnosis. She agrees with me that the first step, however painful it may be for him, should be to show him that though the world is not unsympathetic, it will not obey his every whim. Nobody must give him a penny. We must remember at the same time that he is ill. We must not blame him for his condition or his attitude. She agreed that the best thing for him would be a full course of analysis. But"—and here Amelia laughed pleasantly—"of course Paddy cannot afford that, and Jane, I'm afraid, cannot afford to take on difficult cases for nothing. Until we can arrange to have him treated at a public clinic under the National Health scheme we can do nothing to cure the real cause of his condition. But Jane says that it would be disastrous to aggravate it by encouraging his dependence."

She beamed pleasantly on the table and encouraged McLoosh to another spoonful of friend bananas.

Boddells however was restive. "He should go wandering and wondering in the ways of the world," he said. "He should go like the birreds and the barreds along the roads that twine and twist back on themselves until they bring the homeless beggar home. He should go far away from here."

McLoosh let fall his jaw and a great avalanche of granite growled assentingly down on my head.

"Bee-utiful, bee-utiful, Billy," said Coosins, "and if Paddy is as sick as a dog itself, 'tis the hard road for the sick dog that would maybe be the best cure of all, but 'tis Amelia that knows about the psychiatry and I think the best thing for Paddy would be to get him some small thing to do in the way of a feature on greyhound racing or the like of that and then he could be trotting off to the grand free clinic whenever the fancy took him."

This ambiguous and anxious speech was received in comparative silence. McLoosh let fall another block of granite, though whether in assent or dissent it was hard to say.

"Look at Paddy's clothes," said Amelia. "Paddy probably thinks he dresses like that out of necessity. But I described them to Jane and she said immediately what I thought myself. They are an attempt to call attention to his own inner conflict, not so that he can be helped but so that he will be pitied. You should begin by getting yourself some proper clothes, Paddy. And you should shave every day," she continued severely, gazing short-sightedly at me down the table.

"An old mon I once met in the glens of Ontrim," said Boddells and the company leaned forward expectantly, "An old mon I once met in the glens of Ontrim said to me that it is a sad thing to see a young mon older than his elders. You shouldn't go to ground, Paddy, until you have left the horns and the hounds behind. You should go maybe and join the Foreign Legion like the wild geese that were, or do something desperate and daring that would get you into gaol for a while. When O'Flaherty was your age he was wandering the roads of the world and the rhyme and reason of your situation is that you should do the same."

"Bee-utiful, Billy," said Coosins, "the desperate and daring gaol would be a grand thing. And 'tis Paddy could be writing features about it summer and autumn when he came out, aye, and even for the matter of that while he was in, so that the repeats would be welcoming him like confetti when he came back to us."

"It would be interesting," said the daughter, "to hear from a more or less literate psychopath's own lips whether our present penal system rather gratified his interior wishes and his suppressed grudges than the reverse. My professor certainly thinks it does, and I'm more or less inclined to agree with him."

Amelia and herself discussed the penal system of Soviet Russia with innocence and enthusiasm for a little while. Amelia rather regretted the absence of psychiatry from the course, but was of the opinion that for any such fallings from perfection, the capitalist world, which had hindered the normal development of the revolution, was to blame. Then the attack developed on a new front.

"And you must admit, Paddy," she said, "that as far as any ambitions to being a poet you may have are concerned, your way of life is hardly the best one possible. I mean you are cut off from so much. Money, sex, having a social conscience, routine, discipline—these things are important. We know you live in a doss-house, but you don't seem to have any opinions about it. Your attitude to the social structure is purely detached and selfish."

Fortunately however my socks were evaporating again in the warm atmosphere. The company began to grow restive. McLoosh's great nostrils were quivering. Unable to identify the smell, they were inclined to blame its presence on our hostess who, nervous herself, suggested a removal to another room. There she produced a bottle of whiskey for McLoosh and Boddells and, rather reluctantly, another portion of rough redders for the rest of us. They all sat on the carpet in front of the gasfire, enthusing about a programme of Boddells which had been repeated three times that week, occupying indeed a record number of hours on the ether in any such period: like their conversation, like most of what they admired, it was Celtic, loquacious, adjectival, metaphorical, alliterative, bouncing, lyrical and largely meaningless. Under cover of their enthusiasm and the shaded lighting I succeeded in mixing a dollop of whiskey with my Algerian and busied myself quietly rearranging the figures in a piece of group sculpture beside me. I discovered that instead of being carved out of the same block as the base, they were stuck into it like pocket chess-men, having little marble pins underneath which fitted into holes in the block, and that like chess-men they could be moved around for one's amusement. I was quite happy with this creative task until the party broke up, and profoundly thankful to be no longer the subject of discourse. I knew that my life, the life I had built for myself in recent months, was in ruins, but I was content to be allowed a moment's peace. Then, as we went to the door, the others holding off a little from me, as if fearful that I might jump into their taxi, Amelia took me aside and said kindly, "I want you to come round tomorrow, Paddy, at eleven o'clock sharp. I have something to suggest to you." Thus is one's doom accomplished.

STILL, I might never have gone to Amelia's again, but for the fact that I did not know where else to go. I lay in bed in Coosins' room and considered the matter. My career in the corporation was over, finally over, that was obvious. After last night I could never show my face in the Stork again. I had my sensitivity, and my pride. Yet I had to eat. If I went to Amelia's I might have to suffer another lecture in exchange for a small portion of fried bananas and rice, but after the pain of the previous night the distress would be barely noticeable. Besides, I was curious. I decided to go.

I got there about half-past twelve. Amelia wore a flowered dustcoat and she had in fact been dusting some of the sculpture. I noticed that she flicked over the piece I had rearranged with anxious care, as if to avoid moving any of the figures in their sockets. She reprimanded me for being late. My explanation that I had had to walk was brushed aside as merely further evidence of my neurotic condition.

"Unfortunately, Paddy," she said, "you have succeeded in your object. You have successfully thrown yourself on the mercy of your friends. They have to take some sort of responsibility for you as long as you are sick. But it would be wrong to encourage you to further dependence. All I will do is to help you to help yourself. Neither my conscience nor my knowledge of psychology will allow me to give you something for nothing. If Wally can make a satisfying creative living writing scripts for the corporation, you can. Very well, I will give you the means and the leisure to write those scripts. But you will have to earn it first. Come."

She led me downstairs and through the kitchen into a large garden at the back. We walked to the end of the garden where there was a dark and uncultivated area surrounded by a high wall.

"I want you," she said, "to dig a trench about one and a half feet wide and about two and a half feet deep round the foot of that wall on all three sides and to line the bottom of it with the bricks in that heap. After you have done that you may fill it in again." She must have noticed my expression, for she laughed her light laugh and continued: "Oh no, it isn't pointless therapy. It is a drainage bed for some roses that I want to plant here." I must have been still looking at her, for she hurried on. "Now for every hour's work you do here Paddy, I will give you half a crown. I will also give you a room with a fire in my house to write in every day, and provide you with a hot meal. I'm sure that doss-house you live in is not very suitable for writing. We will think up ideas for feature programmes and you will write synopses under my supervision. If you discipline yourself and do it properly we will have you rehabilitated quite soon. And we can also see about having you treated at a clinic in your, er, spare time. Now there is a spade, Paddy. Would you like to begin?"

I swiftly debated the alternatives in my mind. One was to leave the house instantly, without a penny, and with no place to go to get one. I might endure the correctional treatment at least for a day, and leave the house with seven and a tanner to meditate the next step on. "All right," I said, spitting dolefully on my palms. "I'm game."

It was a cold day in early March and the ground was

rock hard. My progress was slow and would have been slower but for the fact that Amelia fetched out a deck-chair and a rug. There she sat while I worked, and while I worked she lambasted and vilified my character, my achievements and my ways in terms of the fashionable psychology of the day. It was an attack of an unparalleled and atrocious savagery, comprehensive, slanderous and destructive. The fact that it was largely based on guess-work, misinformation and witchcraft did not alleviate the agony of it, for no man likes being abused, accurately or otherwise; and her patient, explanatory lecturer's tone, to say nothing of the exigencies of my work, prevented me from defending myself against truth and falsehood alike. So far from encouraging the worker with popular music, marching songs, or exhortations about the future he was helping to build, Amelia's technique was to destroy him nervously and spiritually by means of a sustained and venomous verbal barrage, based on the writings of Freud and Jung. The technique was effective, for I attacked the frozen ground in a kind of dementia, a compound of despair, fury, terror and sheer self-abasement.

After about four hours we adjourned indoors for some hot cocoa, a fried egg and fried bread—plain, good worker's fare. Then Amelia led me to an apartment at the back of the house, overlooking the accursed garden, simply furnished as a writing-room with a desk, chair, gas-fire and typewriter.

"I want you, Paddy," she said, "to begin by making out a list of possible subjects for feature programmes. I'll get another chair and we can discuss you as we go along."

I explained that whatever about gardening or navvying, I could not write or think except in absolute solitude. This was accepted and Amelia withdrew.

I lay down on the floor in sheer exhaustion of spirit and body and thought about the situation. It is intolerable, I said to myself, and it cannot continue. Of course I was wrong. I think I slept a little. I am not sure. Amelia had warned me not to emerge for at least two hours, so when I woke, if I woke, I decided to give it another little while. There were no books in the room, but there were drawers in the desk. I began to go through them in the hope of coming across something interesting, and indeed I did. Two of them contained Amelia's cancelled and returned cheques, dating back several years, and neatly tied into bundles. After I had been through a bundle or two I discovered that Boddells, McLoosh and one or two other popular and financially successful versifiers of the day had been in receipt of varying but substantial sums from Amelia over the years. I could even imagine the stories that had been told on each occasion: the house-mortgage, the divorce proceedings, the back taxes, even the winter overcoat perhaps, for the amount was sometimes as low as a tenner, though Boddells had once had a monkey and McLoosh had twice had three hundred nicker. Though my experience was no guide, she was certainly a patron. An odd thing was that though Coosins had once had comparatively modest sums every now and then, they appeared to have ceased about two years ago, when I imagined cohabitation to have begun.

Amelia's light knock on the door disturbed me in my researches. When I emerged I explained that I had been so seized with excitement by one idea that I had begun to draft the synopsis, but that I would rather not show it to her till I had worked on it a little more. She accepted this, smiling benignly and murmuring encouragement; presented me with a ten bob note and showed me to the door, reproving me for the state of my shoes and cautioning me to be on time in the morning.

Next morning I awoke in Coosins' little room, racked with pain in every limb and fibre of my physical and mental being. I decided against everything, and for two days I lay and starved. Then Coosins arrived. He told me that Amelia had been around to every Rowton House in London in her Bentley but had drawn a blank everywhere. She was as determined as a bull in a gap and would undoubtedly continue the search until she had combed every Sally and night shelter and inspected every embankment seat. For his sake I must not arouse her suspicions. If she discovered that he had a room he would have to take ship in the service of the French king. For his sake would I go just once more and concoct a story about staying with a friend? She was a woman of great penetration, nearly on the supernatural level, and she was at this moment making enquiries in the Stork. Besides, she had ordered a pick-axe from Harrods and was in a flaming temper because I was not there to justify the expense. She was blaming the whole thing on him.

His fears seemed to me unwarranted and the sacrifice called for very great, but as an act of friendship I went. Amelia was in a huff and led me straight to the pick-axe, a gleaming and patently expensive object, the price of which would undoubtedly have kept me in luxury for a fortnight. She fetched out the rug and the deck-chair and we resumed the therapy. As I swung the pick-axe inexpertly at the hard earth in the thin March sunlight I felt the classic symptoms of hate for the analyst and reflected that so far from lying helpless on a couch I was erect and armed with a weapon providentially supplied by the practitioner herself, but something, as always, held me back. She questioned me closely about where I was staying, and I explained between gasps that I was billeted for the time being with a man called Gudgins, an Irish writer of some distinction who frequented the Stork, but that I would soon have to go back to the Rowton. This seemed to satisfy her and she resumed her assault upon my delicacies and reticencies with savage vigour. After three hours I was a broken man. I could do no more, and we adjourned to the kitchen for some warmed up spaghetti and a blessed bottle of Guinness. Then she produced a new idea. Ignoring my guilty references to the other synopsis she declared that I would write a feature programme about life in a Rowton House. Strictly forbidding me to engage in any other form of composition whatever, she closed the door of the writing room behind me.

I had, needless to say, no notion of exposing my reduced circumstances to the world by taking time on the radio to talk about them; but, since I had not yet had my seven and a tanner, I thought Amelia had better be humoured, and, after a brief rest on the carpet and a brief tour through the cheques, I typed out a number of phrases of the order of "Ashtowk Paddy", "Not since the mother" etc., and explained to her that these would form a sort of chorus, a basic motif, together with the swishing noise of urine being emptied into the buckets, the hawking and spitting of old men and the splintering of skulls. She assented to this idea (rather dubiously I thought), told me I must draw up a proper synopsis tomorrow and dismissed me with my seven and a tanner.

Now, how shall I explain the fact that I returned, and returned again and again for further punishment? It is true that I had nowhere else to go and no other source of income. The thought of the Stork now that the mask had been finally ripped from my face was too awful to contemplate. Nor was what was left of Amelia's daily wage after I had restored my spirits with a drink and another snack really much good for further adventures, hardly enough for bus-fare even, and certainly I could not collect enough capital to tide me over any period of waiting. I had fallen below the first step and the law of the first step was in full operation; but none of this would have mattered—indeed I recognised how craven the reasoning was—except that I believe the combination of physical lassitude and nervous distress which Amelia's methods had induced in me had rendered me, I now think, too helpless to make a break for freedom. I felt I no longer had a right to. I had been reduced to daily slavery as far as what are called practical alternatives are concerned as effectively as if Amelia had bought me in the market; but there was more to it than that: her brain-washing technique was beginning to have its effect.

My days now followed a fairly regular routine. I would wake about ten or eleven in Coosins' little room; don the long flannel trousers, now very much frayed, muddied and torn about the accordion ends from my trenching activities, for Amelia kept me at it in almost all weathers; the broken shoes, now rotting and discoloured from the frequent necessity to work in three or four inches of water; the sportscoat and the off-putting dustcoat; and hurry along to my patroness's. I had secured at least—and it was a big victory in the history of our particular labour relations—the right to a cup of tea before starting work and I sometimes succeeded in getting my teeth into some fried bread and dripping as well. Then down to the trenching, while Amelia, attired for the weather, made herself comfortable in the deck-chair.

She was still in full spate of analysing me, tearing, I imagine, what she thought, God help her, were my defences, pretences and evasions down, and unmasking what she thought were my true motives and motivations, as if I ever had any. Her discourse about me was derogatory, dirty and unfair to a degree, and took of course absolutely no account of the physical and circumstantial obstacles by which I was engulfed, including those of her own devising. Knowing nothing about the law of the first step, having nothing whatever wrong with her that a shower of fivers could cure—for she had uncountable fivers already—Amelia was as intolerant of mere circumstance as a saint. Though rabidly left-wing, she did not seem to realise that there was a general scarcity of cotton plantations. Everybody must pay their way she proclaimed, apparently failing to see that her own ability to do so was not a moral but a circumstantial triumph, for she did, so far as the naked eye could discover, absolutely nothing at all that she did not, in her own sweet way, enjoy doing, while I was at that moment battering away at the yellow earth with my Harrods pick-axe in my hands and tears of indignity and frustration in my eyes. Her moral equations took a bit of juggling before they came out right, for with the disappearance of the factor of private money they were very lopsided, but Amelia was a practised hand at the game and used to ignoring, when it came to laying down the moral law, the fact that some were luckier than others. There was, as far as I could see, wielding my Harrods pick-axe and a new shovel from the Army and Navy Stores through the unsettled days of early April, not much difference between us that could be dignified by any moral terminology, but she had money and I had not. She could avoid working and retain the moral upper hand. I could only try to, if I tried to, but to tell the truth I don't think I ever did. It seems to me now that I have been boasting a bit in this matter. And at that moment was I not wielding a pick and shovel with the best of them? Perhaps I went back to Amelia's because the work she provided me with was the only honest employment that offered? Apart, of course, from the synopses.

The curious thing about Amelia's psychological theories was that they provided her with a basis for believing that one's misfortunes were one's own fault. My particular situation was not due to the law of the first step, nor to the operations of objective reality, but to something in my own nature, in fact a refusal to see the light. She might forgive me for what was, in her opinion, wrong: that, after all, had started in infancy, and though I was, in a way, to blame for embarking on the downward path while still on the potty, I was much more immediately at fault because I would not admit that external circumstances had nothing to do with my present misfortunes, that I was the author of my own doom: me on the potty and me in Amelia's, lapping up the fried bread and dripping, refusing the light that was offered me. How deep and extensive Amelia's knowledge of contemporary psychology may really have been, I do not know. Certainly she paid out enough money to be allowed the privilege of referring to the subject in terms of intimacy; but whether the insensate moral bias in favour of a supposed norm, a norm with enough money in its pocket to pay its way, that she brought to what is, after all, supposed to be a pathology, is a defect in the system itself I cannot say, though I rather suspect, looking back now on her sermons, her denunciations and her vilificatory attitude, that it is. Not to be normal, particularly where money was concerned, was, to Amelia, to be guilty of the sin against the holy ghost. After all, the psychiatrists were prepared to help anybody towards a sensible and responsible attitude towards cash and other matters.

That she managed to combine her psychological theories with her once-fashionable Marxist and fellow-travelling views did not surprise me. It all helped her along, and helped to keep absolutely at bay any compunction there was the slightest risk of her feeling about having inherited the plantation. If she had cash, was she not also a communist? If she had black men working for her, was she not also a progressive? If in her dealing with such as me she had to be perhaps a mite ungenerous, did she not know that my misfortunes were the result of hidden defects in my character, not of mere mischance?

Besides analysing me, she analysed herself and Coosins, whom I briefly and rarely glimpsed about the place, skulking on a landing, or peering from behind a door as I staggered in and out in my muddy pants. He was obviously taking avoiding action. He had several mammoth programmes coming up, including a three-hour feature on leprechauns, and he pleaded the necessity for attendance at the Stork each day, returning only at nightfall to fulfil his duties as man of the house.

Her analysis of herself was pretty favourable. She received encouraging reports of her progress from two or three different schools of thought in return for a number of guineas a week. Only one thing about her seemed to trouble them at the moment, and that was her propensity to give away money. Whatever their differences of opinion in other matters, they were agreed, according to herself at least, that she should not part with a penny to anyone. It set up a feeling of insecurity they said, deep down, and disturbed the careful balance that they were struggling to maintain. The suspicion that she might not be loved for herself alone but only for her yellow gold was inevitable, they concurred, and could bring all her latent insecurities to life once more. I sympathised with their motives at least, though their opinion on this matter was to have rather curious consequences for me.

Her analysis of Coosins was a different matter, but since I regard confidences by either sex about a named person as equally ungallant I struggled not to listen.

The analysing and the digging done we would trot indoors for a quick snack and a session with the synopses. Amelia was almost Irish in her attitude to the B.B.C. and the third programme. It was the magic lodestar towards which she was orientated as completely as any young clod-hopper just off the Liverpool boat. Though she had a wide acquaintance among the literary riff-raff of the day—and indeed of previous days also—her particular friends were Boddells, McLoosh et al., and of course she had Coosins in the house. The synopses were for money, since it was a necessary part of my rehabilitation that I should earn some, but they were creation as well, or designed to lead to it. Her patronage, if that indeed is what I was suffering from, was therefore intended to support me only for the manufacture of synopses, and perhaps the subsequent programmes: not for any other kind of composition, which indeed was strictly prohibited during the hours when I was locked in my little room.

I fear I made but a poor fist of it in spite of all her efforts. She said I had a psychological obstacle to success in that particular quarter, and indeed she was right. I finally put my foot down about the Rowton House idea, pointing out that it is natural for human nature to diminish its degradations and exaggerate the desirability of its circumstances; and that she was asking me to run counter, in the most extreme and public fashion, to this rule. Then when I failed, though locked up for two or three hours every day, to produce other ideas, she produced them for me. I might write features about all-in wrestling, adult education, seals, bird-watching, river conservation, what went on underground in London while we all slept, regency Brighton, and a host of other matters which Amelia's fecund brain thought up.

"The practical discipline of finding out about these things will be good for you," she said, though how I was to find out about anything on seven and a tanner a day was not clear; nor why, if I must write for the accursed radio, and nothing else, I had to confine myself to this sort of dreary journalism.

The synopsising completed in the late afternoon, I would trudge off exhausted. If the pubs were open I would have a beer and a sandwich; otherwise I would make my way to a caff I knew for a cup of tea and a hunk of bread and dripping. Frequently I was too tired and distressed to do more than repair to Coosins' room for a few hours and sit quietly in the local pubs later in the evening. On some occasions I would go exploring other areas, in particular those between Oxford Street and Shaftesbury Avenue. I began, after my diffident fashion, to make acquaintance with pubs and circles other than those in which I had previously spent my days, pubs and circles subtly different indeed from any I had hitherto frequented, from the Stork, from the hostelries of Grafton Street, from O'Turk's even, where other attitudes flourished and other gods were known, where art and a genuine, far below the Gurrier level bucolic indifference, thrived side by side. I did not know it then, for my acquaintance was barely beginning to burgeon, but these were the first steps on a road that was to lead me to a freedom which was both above in one sense and below in another the circumstantial necessities and social respects which, it seems to me now, had hitherto enthralled me, even in the O'Turk's days. But that was in the future. My acquaintance was too limited at the moment for me to understand that here was a sea upon which I could cast my bread. For the moment I was Amelia's synopsising and pick-axe wielding slave, and both of us knew it.

I can give no coherent account I am afraid of the synopsis manufacturing. Amelia had succeeded in gaining entrance to the room with me while I worked, so that I could no longer even lie on the floor or commune with the cancelled cheques. We must have struggled through at least one, myself in a sort of trance-like state, for subsequent developments were to show that at least one was manufactured, but I have no memory of it.

This went on for three or four weeks. Then one morning Coosins came to the room before I was up.

"Paddy my boocal," he said, "I want you to hurry on now with the synopses and with the programmes that will follow as surely as the night the day. At least give Amelia every help you can in the writing of them, for with all her great brain 'tis you that has the nicer turn of phrase."

I averred that I was a broken man, long past caring about synopses or anything else.

"I will tell you why I ask, Paddy," he went on anxiously. "Amelia is behaving very strangely towards her old and trusted and tried and true friends. Neither Billy nor Caspar can get a penny out of her in any circumstances whatever, though they're both in great need at the moment. It is known that you are seeing a great deal of her, and she has said in the Stork that she is rehabilitating you and providing you with the time and the money to go on writing until the repeats start. Feeling is running very high against you, Paddy. 'Tis said that you have no right to go begging and cadging like that from her, and you without a programme or a repeat to your name. I have done my best to explain that what you get wouldn't put herrings on the potatoes, but I don't want to say too much in that direction either, for they wouldn't think it respectable of you to be so reduced, and if the word got round the corporation that you were digging a ditch for her like a navvy it wouldn't help you to be rolling the words over the broad road of the radio either."

I explained as clearly as I could that my interest in the radio was at a low ebb.

"Whisht up now Paddy and don't be talking like that at all," said Coosins warmly, "for 'tis the grand life it is with the repeats and the programmes playing leap-frog with each other summer and autumn. Besides, Paddy, to tell you the truth feeling is beginning to turn against me too, and the rumours that are flying round are not doing me any good at all in certain influential circles. I have tried to get Amelia to say it's only a very small sum she is giving you, but 'tis not in her her nature I don't think, and anyway I don't know which of them would be the worst, the truth or the falsehood, the hundreds or the navvying. Sometimes I'm in dread and terror that she'll tell them the truth and that wouldn't do any good either."

I was still not just exactly clear how hurrying on with the synopses would help.

"Well you see, Paddy, the only sure way they have to

know in the Stork whether a man is earning any money or not is by the announcements in the *Radio Times*, and if it was seen that you were earning a bit for yourself there would be less cause for resentment. They'd have to give best to you on that score anyway. They could no longer say that you were living entirely off Amelia. You see at the moment 'tis down on you they'll be whether 'tis hundreds or ha'pence you're getting and I'm in a red flush of embarrassment about the whole thing myself."

I could sense an obscure logic in this and I promised to use my heaven-sent opportunity to produce as many synopses as possible.

Hardly had Coosins gone when there came a tapping on the door. It was one of the German ladies who lived downstairs, "Are you Mr. Riley? " she asked. "Well there iss somebody vants to speak to you on the telephone."

There was a telephone in the hallway, but nobody had ever rung me up, since, apart from my general anonymity, my presence in the house was supposed to be a dark secret between Coosins and myself. I struggled into my muddy pants and jacket and went downstairs. To my horror, the voice on the telephone was Amelia's.

She accused me of treachery and disloyalty to my only true friend in the world. "I found this telephone number in Wally's little book. I knew very well you were not staying in a Rowton House. Confess to me immediately that Wally pays for that room. I knew he had a room somewhere. I knew it."

I denied everything, saying that the room was mine. "Absolute nonsense. You can't pay for a room out of what I give you. Come round here immediately."

I trudged around. Amelia met me at the door. She was solemn and grave. She brought me into the room where the sculpture was, sat me down and offered me coffee and cigarettes.

"Let me tell you about my relationship with Wally," she began. "I want to talk to you quite seriously about it."

I didn't want to hear, but it was better than the digging or the subject of me.

"Wally is Irish," she said, "and everybody knows how puritanical the Irish are. You know yourself. In the early days of our relationship he was deeply, immaturely and puritanically shocked at the thought that he was having an affair with a woman a certain number of years older than himself. Not consciously of course, he would have denied that, but subconsciously. Therefore he felt a subconscious need to regard me as a mother figure, and he also felt a subconscious need to defy and mock and disobey that mother figure behind her back. That is why he had affairs with other women: not that he found them more attractive than he found me, because I know myself that I fulfil Wally completely sexually, but to change the nature of his subconscious guilt and to transfer it on to another plane. His guilt was now that of outraging the mother. Both greater and lesser. A typical puritanical reaction. Being Irish, if you are honest with yourself you will understand perfectly. I knew that he had kept a room to conduct these affairs in even after he had moved in here. It was an immature phase of our relationship which, under my guidance, I hoped he would outgrow. I believe he has outgrown it. I believe the only reason he has kept that room on was out of friendship for you. I found in his pockets this morning a letter from some creature saying she had rung a certain Swiss Cottage number several times, but he was never there. It was the number I had found in his book. This made me suspicious. I rang that number. I asked for Wally. He was not there. The woman asked if I would like to speak to the other gentleman. It was you. You. I remembered when I searched all the Rowton Houses in London and failed to find you. You were there. That is the only reason why Wally has kept that room on. To help you. I know it. You have been there all the time. Confess."

I confessed. I tried to explain that I had genuinely been in a Rowton House, but she interrupted me gravely and severely.

"Paddy, you shock me very deeply," she said. "And I thought we had produced some improvement in you. In the first place you have been taking my money under false pretences. When I gave you money each day I was under the impression that you had to pay for a night's lodging out of it. You have been dishonest with me, and you have also been dishonest with your friends, who have been under the impression that you were living in a doss-house, and on whose sympathy and interest in sociology you have accordingly been able to trade. Probably your dishonesty with me was an attempt to prove that what I said about your psychological state was not true, since in the end you were cleverer than I was and able to score over me. Very probably each time you dishonestly took my money was a subconscious victory over my advice and my analysis of your character. I understand all that, but there is something else that I find it hard to understand. In the course of helping you I have come to like you. I thought that apart from being merely grateful you had come to like me. That we were truly friends. And now I find that you stab me in the back by forcing Wally out of his weakness and generosity to keep on that room, so that at any moment he may have a . . . a relapse."

She looked at me in silence and in sorrow. I looked down at my blistered hands, but I had no words of defence. I was consumed with admiration.

She sighed, as if wearily gathering her strength after yet another betrayal, and when she spoke again her voice, for all its undertone of sorrow, was firm.

"Wally must give that room up, Paddy. He must give it up today. I am going down to the B.B.C. now to find him. In the meantime I want you to get on with the rose-bed."

When I heard the Bentley go I came back into the house to look for a drink. I found a bottle of whiskey and a siphon and I sat down in the front room and moved the figures around in their sockets for a while. I worked out that I was being paid, between the digging and the synopses, about one and threepence an hour. I was resigned to that, if you can call the state of mind I was in resigned, though I was being driven like a nigger for six hours a day and it is well known that the combination of physical and mental work is the hardest of all. But would I be able to keep going? I had practically given up drinking, but I could scarcely travel and eat and keep up my strength on the five bob or so I would have left after forking out for the Rowton, let alone have a bitter here and there to make new acquaintances. I took another swig of whiskey. I was beginning to be relieved and elated by the clear-cut impossibility of the whole thing. I went and communed with the cancelled cheques for a while. The evil stirrings of ambition, that remorse in advance that we feel when we are about to blight a so-called opportunity, were absent. I took a cheque which had once been made out to Boddells in the sum of three hundred pounds as a memento. I burned what synopses, or fragments of synopses, I could find; made a parcel out of the whiskey bottle and the siphon; and left the house. It was high April, verging on May, and warm in the side-roads of Hampstead. I had absolutely no place to go.